I0526550

Wylder Opal

by

Maryanne Ross

The Wylder West Series

Wylder Opal

Cover Art by *Tina Lynn Stout*

The Wild Rose Press, Inc.
PO Box 708
Adams Basin, NY 14410-0708
Visit us at www.thewildrosepress.com

Publishing History
First Edition, 2023
Trade Paperback ISBN 978-1-5092-4695-3
Digital ISBN 978-1-5092-4696-0

The Wylder West Series
Published in the United States of America

"Men come to the frontier because they have secrets, sweetheart."

Ooh. *Sweetheart.* In a gritty, gravelly voice that skittered over her skin.

She tilted her left shoulder forward and pouted her lips. "Don't you know better than to tempt a woman with the mention of *secrets*?"

He laughed, white teeth gleaming under his long black moustache, dark eyes flashing with amusement. "Crikey! Played that badly." With that smile, his whole face lit, changing from thunder to sweet spring sunshine. "Not safe out here for pretty hothouse flowers."

She jutted her chin. "I'm no hothouse bloom. I'm a gunslinger."

He choked. His lips pressed tight. Then he released a huge belly laugh, long-fingered hands pressing into his thighs as he bent forward.

She slammed her right hand on her hidden holstered hip, mean-eyed. She tapped an impatient toe. Men always underrated her, always tried to coddle and hedge her in. Even her tall, fierce sharpshooter brothers did sometimes. Not for long.

Opal drew her Smith & Wesson .44 Russian with a smooth, quick motion even her daddy would have approved and shot a metal mug off a stump thirty yards away.

He dropped his pick, which clanged to the rocky ground and held both hands up in surrender. "Stone the flamin' crows! Feisty damsel. A man'd be a fool to cross you." He shot a quick look back at his damaged cup. Quirked a black brow. A grin creased the corners of his lips.

Praise for Maryanne Ross

Praise for Crushing the Corset

"…awesome romance. Page-turner, romantic, unpredictable, witty, wonderful characters."
~ 5 stars, Brenda, BookBub

"A feisty, beautiful heroine in need for rescue - check, an outlaw hero helping her - check, a wicked villain plotting against our heroine - check. The book is intriguing, interesting and will keep your attention focused on the plot from the first sentence you read. It is definitely worth your time."
~ 5 stars, Netgalley reviewer

Praise for Bouncing the Bustle

"…an immense pleasure to read…storytelling, characters and vivid descriptions are captivating."
~ Neeha, Reedsy

"…definitely recommend this to my friends."
~ Hani, Netgalley

Dedication

To my father, James Ross, who asked for a romance-western. With love and thanks for a lifetime of stories!

Wylder author acknowledgements

Wylder West is a shared world.
A big shout out to all the other Wylder authors, and especially those authors whose wonderful characters appear in *Wylder Opal*: Talia Logan (Sheriff Branch Wylder), Nicole McCaffrey, and Sarita Leone, April Hollingworth (Molly Maguire & Parkinson), Barb Bettis (newspaper editor), Renee Johnson (postmistress), and Tena Stetler (blacksmith).

A special huge thank you to Laura Strickland for lending Buck and Cissy Standish, and to Marilyn Barr for the riotous Sagebrush family and the bear cub.

Chapter One

Early May, 1880

Opal Calahan was handy with a gun—and even handier with a pen. Her new Plan galloped in her mind, as lively as the antelope racing the train. She jiggled her legs under cover of her skirts. Come on, *come on*!

"Last stop, Wylder." The conductor lifted down her carpetbag and valise from the luggage rack. "What might you be doing way out here in the Wild West, all by yerself, miss?"

"I'm trackin' a gunslinger."

The man stared, pop-eyed, and almost dropped her valise. The train whistle hooted, and her belly clenched with excitement.

On the facing seat, the sleeping mound of disarrayed clothing, lip-paint, and curls stirred and sat up. "Plenty of sharpshooters in Wylder, my lovely. Cowboys and outlaws too."

The conductor smoothed his moustache. "Dangerous men, miss."

Opal slid him a wink. "One particular gunslinger will do."

He shook his head and turned away muttering, his walk a practiced dance with the rocking of the train.

The two women stared at each other. Opal pointed to her own cheek to show where a smear of lip paint

1

had escaped. The woman said, "And why—"

Urgent words swirled in Opal's brain and burst out like the hot steam from the train. "After I find my gunfighter…" She sucked in a couple of quick breaths while her companion drew out a hand mirror.

Could she own her dream, say it out loud to a stranger? "I'm gonna be…Wylder's newest and best playwright!"

The woman's bright eyes fixed on Opal. She raised her arched brows encouragingly.

Opal waved her arms. "In plays—if my characters accidentally misspeak, if they act too fiery or hasty, I can write them a second chance."

Her companion nodded. "Lovely! You'll be Wylder's only playwright, far as I know. Good luck to you, my sweet."

With a conversation-drowning roar and great plume of thick smoke, the train pulled into Wylder railway station. Opal disembarked into a warm spring breeze, gripping her luggage as her train companion shouted directions in her ear. "Go up Sidewinder Lane there, with the honky-tonk bar on the corner."

She swung her bags to tinkling piano music issuing from the saloon as she headed up the narrow lane. At last, Wylder Street! Opal stepped up into the lobby of the grand Vincent House Hotel, luxuriating in the welcome embrace of cool air, clean-scented with vinegar and wax.

"Dollar fifty per night or seven dollars per week, Miss Calahan."

She grimaced at the eye-watering tariff but quickly pretended she merely squinted at the clerk's name tag. "Two weeks. Thank you, James."

In her pretty room, she made a lightning-fast wash and change and headed off on an exploratory walk to stretch muscles stiff from travel.

Opal edged through gun-toting cowboys in woolen vests, the air humming with male laughter. She dodged clip-clopping buggies, fringed surreys, and steaming horse poop. A side alley lured her down past the fancy Wylder County Social Club, with its fretwork balconies and a red lamp glowing at its door.

A footbridge beckoned over a glittering river. She strode out across the town's scrabbly, desert-chewed edges. Herb-scented air tickled her nose. Jagged mountains soared in blues and grays on the skyline.

She rounded a curve in the track and stopped, stunned.

Best of all?

Right now, she just might have found her perfect leading man.

A broad-shouldered, dusty-garbed man held a long-handled pick high overhead, then slammed it down in a rhythmic thumping stroke into the rocky river bank. The lean muscles in his sweat-damp shirt—back and arms—flexed and pulsed with the action. His worn cotton trousers hung low on lean hips. A tanned hand flicked back a sweat-soaked curl.

Opal swallowed, transfixed. *What was he doing?* She darted a quick glance around. Shallow metal bowls with mesh bottoms were scattered along the riverbank. Some kind of sluice contraption stood in the burbling stream.

Did she gasp aloud? He sensed her presence and whirled, body alert, his pick wielded before him like a weapon.

Whew, reflexes! A smoldering dark gaze nailed her.

Had she found the gunslinger then? Tough. Calm. Self-contained. Devastatingly handsome. Tall, with that special athletic balance...just as she had imagined him.

Better be sure. "What's your name, mister?"

She repressed a fidget as a long silence stretched. His gravel voice uttered, "Heath."

Oh. Not the gunslinger. A knife of disappointment lanced her. "Heath? Well, that's pretty."

He snorted. Muttered "pretty" under his breath. Curled his lip as if she'd said something ridiculous.

She waited, trading stare for stare. She couldn't hold out. "What's your other name?"

"No other name." He leaned on his long-handled pick.

Did he have a strange kind of accent? Fascinated, she probed. "Your surname. Family name. Ya can't be just Heath!" She smiled to take the bossy sting from the words.

He scratched his stubbled jaw, skewering her with a smoldering dark glare. "Why do you want to know?"

Definitely an accent. Sort of flat and musical at the same time, somehow with sun and wildflowers woven in. "I'm curious, is all. What's the big deal?"

"Men come to the frontier because they have secrets, sweetheart."

Ooh. *Sweetheart*. In a gritty, gravelly voice that skittered over her skin. A little bit dazzled by all that manliness.

Stop that. This heart is occupied already.

She tilted her left shoulder forward and pouted her lips. "Don't you know better than to tempt a woman with the mention of *secrets*?"

He laughed, white teeth gleaming under his long black moustache, dark eyes flashing with amusement. "Crikey! Played that badly." With that smile, his whole face lit, changing from thunder to sweet spring sunshine.

Crikey. What was that? She stored the expression away in her word-hungry brain. She pressed her advantage. "C'mon. Tell. Pleeeeease?"

"And then you'll go? Not safe out here for pretty hothouse flowers."

"Now, why would I do that? We've only just met! I'm fine, anyhow." She jutted her chin. "I'm no hothouse bloom. *I'm a gunslinger.*"

He choked. His lips pressed tight. Then he released a huge belly laugh, long-fingered hands pressing into his thighs as he bent forward.

She slammed her right hand on her hidden holstered hip, mean-eyed. She tapped an impatient toe. Men always underrated her, always tried to coddle and hedge her in. Even her tall, fierce sharpshooter brothers did sometimes. Not for long.

Opal drew her Smith & Wesson .44 Russian with a smooth, quick motion even her daddy would have approved and shot a metal mug off a stump thirty yards away.

He dropped his pick, which clanged to the rocky ground and held both hands up in surrender. "Stone the flamin' crows! Gunslinger, hey. Feisty damsel. A man'd be a fool to cross you." He shot a quick look back at his damaged cup. Quirked a black brow. A grin creased the corners of his lips.

He bowed. "Heath Rawdon. At your service." He

raked her with that dark gaze. "I apologize for laughing. You look way too dainty and sweet to pack a gun."

"Well, you'd be wrong."

The silence clanged between them. Opal wrenched her rioting brain back to her mission in Wylder. "Know a man called Buck Standish?"

Heath Rawdon blinked. His forehead creased. "Why do you want to know?"

"He humiliated my little brother, Neddy. Also a gunfighter." Well, that was part of the truth.

Heath curled his lip again. "You'll probably find him back in town. But you'd better leave that Buck Standish alone, if you ask me."

"I didn't ask you." Opal tossed her head.

With a few quick, graceful movements, he stacked his tools neatly by the tent. He bundled a small package into a leather pouch. Dusted his hands on his pants. Those hands. Calm. Gunslinger steady.

He held one out. "Here, I'll walk you back to town. These mountains are wild and lonely. Even a gun-toting, fire-breathing wench shouldn't be out here by herself."

Opal snickered. "I wouldn't want to keep you from your work, mister." But he came anyway.

"What are you up to out here, Mr. Heath Rawdon?"

He slowed his long-legged, loose stride to match her pace. His large frame blocked the gritty wind snatching at her skirts.

"Hiding from the world." His mouth twisted. A tiny silvered knife scar twitched on his left cheekbone. "Heath. Drop the Rawdon."

"Hmm. Doesn't hiding involve keeping a low profile, not slamming noisy picks around and scattering

6

one's belongings from river to mountain?"

How she loved his laugh! So rumbling and infectious, but rusty, as though long disused.

He avoided a direct answer. Instead, he grated, "I'll thank you to keep my name and my activities to yourself, Miss Gunslinger."

She realized—he hadn't asked her name. Frontier courtesy? Or lack of interest?

And why did she care?

They traded snappy banter all the way to the bridge into town. At the town border, Heath nodded once, spun on his heel and left.

She stood, blinking in the warm sun, until she pulled herself together.

As she bustled up the road to the Vincent House Hotel, a man in a sheriff's uniform stepped in front of her. Two holstered 1873 Colt Single Action revolvers rode high on his hips. Nice.

"New in town, miss? You best stay away from that fellow," he said, jerking his chin toward the bridge. He tipped his hat at her. "Branch Wylder, sheriff of these parts."

"Oh? Opal Calahan, sir…playwright."

"That so? Well, that man might inspire an interesting character. But it's my job to listen to whispers—and I've heard tell that mountain loner is a wanted man. Price on his head. Claim jumping. Bushranging. Murder. Don't want to brand a man unfairly—I'm making inquiries."

A hot surge of denial surprised her. But the lawman was only doing his job. "I thank you, Sheriff. I'll keep that in mind." She gave him her sunniest smile and traipsed on to her hotel.

Rats! She should ask him if her triggerman was in town. She swiveled.

The sheriff stood straight-backed, right hand resting on his Colt, staring out toward the mountains. Oh. Better leave him be.

A thrill ran through her. Frontier town. Danger. Excitement. Her steps picked up.

At the lovely Vincent Hotel, she had a quick wash in her sweet room, brushed down her dress, and tidied her hair. The housekeeper, Molly Maguire, brought in warm water and fresh towels and lingered. "Don't mind our resident ghosts now, Miss Calahan. They won't hurt you any."

Wow! Hotel ghosts. She adored Wylder already. Which was all to the good if her plans for the famous gunfighter worked, and she was to stay here.

As Mrs. Buck Standish. Playwright.

Stepping out of hotel, Opal enacted imaginary scenes of her first sight of her hero, Buck Standish. In her fantasy, romantic violin music soared as their gazes locked in instant passion in a dusty Western street.

No, that wasn't right. Those dark satiric eyes belonged to the prospector. And that dark brown curling hair. And that lanky, muscular body. Calahan, take a breath and start again.

Now she didn't know what her imaginary Buck looked like. His physical presence—described so many times by his adoring little sister Abbigail—had wavered and vanished. Opal frowned.

"Excuse me," she said, turning back to the Vincent Hotel doorman. "Is the famous gunslinger Buck Standish in town?"

One hairy gray eyebrow twitched. "You might try

the bakery just across the street, miss."

The bakery?

Well, she supposed even renowned gunsharks had to eat.

Opal dodged a thundering coach spraying dust, two mounted cowboys, and a herd of noisy, scruffy boys kicking a ball. She wandered across to the bakery, still frowning.

The warm, yeasty smell of fresh-baked pies and breads wafted enticingly. A vivid-faced woman with lovely white-blond hair piled high smiled at her as she arranged a tray of dainty cakes in the window.

The patrons included two giggling, wiggling women with low-cut dresses and painted faces—had she found Wylder's actresses? Four men, all sturdy, all wearing hard-worn gear, waited in broody, hungry silence for their pies. But the men lacked that special light-footed balance of the dedicated gunslinger. She should know. Her daddy and three brothers were gunfighters. Well, two of her brothers. Her baby brother Neddy…

Which brought her mission slamming into her brain.

Damn that handsome prospector, making a girl giddy and forgetful.

"Can I help you?" The pretty blonde's voice was as charming as her hair.

"I'm looking for…" Now it came to it, her words dissolved on her tongue. She'd spent months dreaming about Buck Standish, weaving her plans, visualizing their dramatic meeting.

Opal cleared her throat. "…Buck Standish? The famous gunslinger."

"Oh yes? And who wants to know?" A hint of steel rang in that sweet voice.

A tall man bustled out from the kitchen, heaving a tray of delicious-smelling pies. His floral, frilly apron emphasized the strength in his arms. Opal didn't miss the adoring glance he cast at her companion.

Opal said, "I wanted to talk to him about my little brother, Ned Calahan. Buck totally humiliated him in a gunfight."

The tray wobbled. A pie slid. The apron-clad man snapped out a lightning-fast hand and caught it deftly, balancing the tray in the other hand.

Despite the warmth from the kitchen, palpable cool emanated from the woman now. The pie catcher stood frozen.

"I wanted to thank him. For saving my foolish brother's life." A tear squeezed itself down Opal's cheek. "The famous Buck Standish could have killed him, easy, and instead, he just…he just fired into…and I was looking for Buck to thank him, and found his sister Abbigail, and now we are friends!" she finished in a torrent of words. "And Abbigail talked of her brother so often, in such glowing terms—"

I fell in love with him.

The platinum-haired woman wrapped Opal in a hug, rubbing her back with slow, soothing strokes. Opal sobbed into her shoulder for a moment, and then wiped her swollen eyes and salt-stung cheeks with her crumpled handkerchief. "Sorry, sorry."

"I'm Cissy, and Buck Standish is my husband," the woman said quietly. "A finer man never walked this earth." The man in the apron and Cissy gazed dotingly at each other.

"Abbigail? I'd love to hear news of my little sister," Buck said in a deep voice.

My husband. Opal's world shattered and splintered. A voice roared in her head that she was all kinds of fool. "Later!" she managed to squeak. "Thank you!" she gasped at Cissy, and dashed headlong from the bakery, every instinct bent on flight.

Married! Her hero, Buck Standish, was married.

All her plans for so many long months. Vanished. Gone. Ridiculous. Impractical, mad, ill-informed, impulsive. *Hasty.*

Opal race-walked down unfamiliar streets and narrow, dusty lanes, barely registering her surroundings. It wouldn't do to cry in this strange place, in public. Bad enough embarrassing herself in the bakery, in front of half the town.

"Put it in a play. Don't get mad, or upset, or shamed. Have a character enact it in a play instead." Maybe the whirling wind made her eyes sting and her cheeks wet.

Rough gravel crunched underfoot. Dust and flying grit whipped her cheeks, bringing scents of sagebrush and mineral soils. She put a hand to her eyes—and took in her location. Low foothills exploded sharply into mountains. The sky hung in a huge opalescent dome. She'd walked to the edge of town and over the bridge.

Whoops.

The sheriff had warned her.

But here she was.

Chapter Two

The mountain loner burst from a deep square mineshaft in the ground, like Hades, the terrifying god of the underworld. She shrieked and jumped backward, stumbling on rubble.

She righted herself quickly as his arm reached for her. She jerked away. A woman had her pride.

She was alone in the foothills of a frontier town. With a wanted man. Tall, strong, fit—and glowering. Potential weapons everywhere: rocks, steel picks, metal thingies.

She slapped a hand on her gun, tucked against her hip.

Heath threw his hands in the air, dark eyes glinting. His white teeth glimmered in a grin. "A woman in tears, going for her weapon. More dangerous than a tiger snake, or whatever serpents you have out here."

There was that accent again, one she'd never heard before. Kind of flat, but full of sunshine and humor for all that. Magnetized, she stepped closer.

He studied her. "Here, sit down. Catch your breath. That heaving bosom is way too distracting." She clapped a hand to her breast, outrage drying her tears. The left half of his mouth flirted with a smile. He picked up a flask. "Have a swig—hot tea."

She cautiously reached out a hand. Hesitated. Alone in the foothills with a wanted man. This close, she could smell clean working man, washed cotton, a hint of leather and soap—and a spicy tang of fresh sweat. Quite a heady elixir.

For some mad reason, she trusted him. She sensed a steadiness deep within him that offered an anchor for her fizzy nature. She took a drink.

Opal choked and sputtered. "What the hell? Is that half tea, half whiskey?"

He did fully grin now. That charming, cheeky smile did something to her stomach, which somersaulted. And to her toes, which curled in her boots.

"Only way to drink it, isn't it?" His deep voice softened. Manly concern wrapped around her like a prickly tweed rug. "What happened to you, lovely? I hate to see those tears…"

And then, who knew, maybe she should've eaten one of Cissy's pies after all, maybe she was weak with hunger, because suddenly her story came pouring out—without mentioning names.

He listened calmly until her rush of words slowed to a miserable, embarrassed trickle.

"So you've spent months hankering after a man you never met." He inhaled audibly. "You thought you loved him."

She sat bolt upright and snapped, "I did love him. The feeling itself is genuine, isn't it?" Did he think her a desperado? She added quickly, "Had plenty of offers. Just no man measured up to my gunslinger." She tossed her head and sneaked a peek at his reaction.

His lean, hard body leaned closer. His coffee eyes seared her. "You intended to marry a sharpshooter. A hired gun. That's what you want? That dangerous, short, violent gunfighter life?"

"Ye—" The full meaning of his words suddenly penetrated. Shock sizzled through her body as a revelation hit. Golden flashes lit in her brain. Her mouth popped open in stunned surprise. "I'm *very* good at shooting. But deliberately harming people? That's so different. One time I went on a job with Burnley, my older brother—"

She pressed her mouth shut.

"Yes?"

"…never mind."

She took his hand, his warmth and the roughness of his tool-abraded palm anchoring her while she thought this new concept through.

She rubbed his fingers. "You are right. Even for the best—and we Calahans *are* the best—the gunslinger life is short and ugly. If I leave that life, I can save my baby brother. He could've died…" Fresh tears erupted. She released his hand to cover her face with her own.

He tugged her hands down. Gentle fingertips soothed her burning tears away. "Who is the lucky man?" His voice scratched hoarse. A pulse jumped in his cheek.

She licked her lips. May as well confess the lot. Let him laugh. "Buck Standish."

"The *baker*?"

She hunched a shoulder. Must he sound so incredulous?

The gravel in his voice turned to flint. "A fine man, but he belongs heart and soul to Mrs. Cissy Arkwright Standish."

Opal flashed back, voice humming low, cross with herself all over again, "Yes, my imagination is always

14

big and bright. I'm always inventing stories and yarns."

He didn't mock. His dark brows snapped together. "That attitude can get you killed. Or perhaps the fairies protect you. They look after fools and children."

Ooh, that hurt! But with all her tough brothers, it took a rare man to intimidate Opal. She rallied. "How romantic," she retorted, sugar sweet. "Do you seek the wee folk out here yourself, in these rocks you smash?"

He speared her with a gunpowder stare. "I've no time for fiction. There's only what you can see in front of your eyes, what you can clutch in your fist. Look where making up stories has got you."

She kicked a lump of rock. Time to change the subject. "What *are* you doing out here, anyway?" She gazed out at the red plains and inhaled the dusty-green scent of sagebrush. A tinge of fresh pine floated from the distant mountains.

Temper mounted in his cheeks, and his lips firmed. He growled, "I'm a prospector. Looking for gold. Jade. Opal."

She smiled.

"What are you smirking at?"

"Well…you found her." She stuck out her hand, all pert business. "I'm Opal Calahan. At your service." Yikes. That could be misconstrued.

She tensed.

But he was distracted by her name. Heath rumbled, "Don't you know opals are well-known to bring bad luck?"

She could keep him talking all day. That accent. Those shoulders. That sizzling dark stare. He made her tingle all over, like the cymbal crash in a play's pivotal moment.

15

She fluttered her damp eyelashes at him. "Doesn't stop you searching."

He said, gruff-toned, "Opals are among the most beautiful jewels." He stopped.

"Yes?"

"In a gold setting, an opal with a milky shine like your skin...with blue-turquoise fire just like your eyes, as changeable as Lady Fortune...There's magic in opals, swirling in their depths."

Well! Where had her breath gone, when she needed it to snap a retort? Or her quick brain, for that matter?

Gratitude swirled through her, soft in her stomach. "Well, you've unearthed a jewel for me today. You birthed a revelation sparkling in my brain. My little setback with Buck is not a roadblock but an open gate. My Wonderful Plan just morphed into an Even More Fabulous Plan, rated priority." She took both his hands and squeezed. "Thank you."

His dark brows furrowed. "Plan? Why am I filled with unease?" His large, calloused hands still wrapped hers.

"I'm not marrying a gunslinger. Now, I can escape that chancy life." She could bring her baby brother to Wylder, before he—

Opal would save them both; she *must* become that playwright, sooner rather than later.

She leaned in, wallowing in Heath's rangy size, his muscular strength and man-scent: leather, fresh sweat, and desert sage, both comforting and thrilling.

Her lips hovered near his. Touched. She tasted heat and desire. His mouth slid over hers. Desperate fingers clutched her shoulders and pulled her in for a brief, heavenly moment.

16

He released her, hands flying up. He coughed and shifted sideways. A growl rumbled deep in his throat. His face turned away, a pulse beating in his tanned neck.

She said to his left ear, words tumbling and urgent, "I'm following my star. I'm gonna be Wylder's newest and best playwright!"

He leaped to his feet, his entire frame stiff with outrage. A pang of unease smote her for the first time. This prospector seemed mighty moody. Unpredictable.

Sometimes she could tease her brothers from moodiness. Sometimes teasing made them crankier. He needed to lighten up.

Opal stood up and strolled around him, eyeing him like a rancher checking the cattle, enjoying herself. "I need a man who can stand on the stage and glower. Yes, exactly like that." She'd write the part first thing.

He shook his head, radiating fury. That strong jaw clenched tight. White-knuckled fists clamped on his thighs. What was his problem?

"With that charming accent, what about just one or two teensy words for the stage?"

"How about *no*?"

"Mmm. Doesn't quite work for me. Got any others?"

He glared. "What are you doing out here again? In the lonely sky and hills? Go back to the safe streets in town, Miss Calahan." He stalked over to his tools and pulled up his pick.

"Harsh!" She stood her ground. She cut a wary glance to her escape route and rested a hand on her gun.

Maybe she should feel scared, out here, alone with him.

But she didn't. Not at all.

She said, "Funny. Maybe it's a flaw—I've always preferred wild to civilized. The frontier to tiny streets, mad hotels to neat-kept houses."

She had his interest now. He threw down his pick and took two paces toward her.

Then she ruined it. "How did you like my speech? It's for one of my characters, Maryann."

Disgusted, he turned away, muttering, "That's the problem with the world. Everyone pretends."

The prospector turned back and raked her with a moody, unfathomable gaze. Words jerked from him. "How about you go dancing with a real man?"

Her eyes widened. She looked him up and down. Oh yes. Here was a real man, all right.

While her mind whirled—yes, no, you don't know him, what could happen in the middle of town, the sheriff won't be happy—her mouth opened. "Yes," it said.

Her eyes opened wide. A visceral flash of dancing, held against that strong, fit body, within those muscular arms, slammed into her brain. A hot sizzle of thrill raced over her skin.

The creases around his mouth deepened. Shadows gathered on his temples. Desire? Pain? Triumph? Secrets, for sure.

"What dance?" she asked. "When?"

His face shuttered. "The very next time there's a dance or shindig in this town that time forgot, I'd be proud to escort you."

She swallowed a ping of disappointment. She would ask at the Vincent House Hotel about the next Wylder dance...

And he'd given away a clue—*land that time forgot.* Did he hail from fancier streets than these? And his accent—a good education lurked in the shape and choice of his words.

His next words rumbled through her. His dark eyes looked suddenly vulnerable, uncertain. "Perhaps you would enjoy a picnic tomorrow, out here in the wild? As you seem to enjoy visiting."

Picnic? Lure the damsel, then indulge in a spot of pillage and murder? A stage villain's wicked laughter rang in her ears. Nobody would know what had happened to her, if she suddenly vanished. They'd conclude she'd just skipped town.

How could she trust her own judgement after today's bakery debacle? *Hasty.* Her brothers' scornful, concerned voices rang in her ears.

"Perfect!" her mouth answered, apparently quite unconnected to her brain. Heat slid over her skin like a warm, gentle palm.

She tugged her gaze from his fingers. Her brain rapidly calculated options. "Here's the deal. I'll come— if you'll show me a little about prospecting. About searching for gold, or jade." That might be the closest he'd come to talking about himself. He might let another clue slip.

The man fascinated her. And a gem would certainly be welcome, to help finance her dream. Now she was a single woman.

He quirked a heavy brow and nodded.

She bubbled, "I'll bring pies from Cissy's bakery. And proper tea!"

Heath walked with her until they were in sight of the bridge leading into town.

"I don't know why you worry," she said, laughing up at him. "Aren't you the only wild man out here?"

His nostrils flared. "Tomorrow," he said grimly.

As though they'd arranged a duel, rather than a picnic.

****

What was he thinking?

Heath smacked his pick hard into the seam of quartz running into the clay along the river bank. Alluvial gold. All the indicators were present. Different river, different skies, different *hemisphere,* but the same thread of gold-specked quartz which promised riches.

She'd appeared like a vision, like some kind of flower of the desert, springing up strong and utterly pretty after the first rains. Exquisite. Tempting.

Standing there with her cloud of frizzy brown hair, as though it heated from her bright and active mind, and turquoise-aqua eyes as mysterious and magical as opals. That pointed chin and cheeky, teasing grin, matching her slender, elfin frame.

She could distract a man from his caution. From his carefully curated loneliness and isolation. Even from his raging gold-hunger.

He leaned on his pick, squinting up into the bright desert sky. A lone golden eagle hovered high, then swooped down for its prey.

One picnic with her.

Then it had to stop. He couldn't afford another— his mind clamped down. A shrilling whistle screamed in his ears. Swirling darkness fogged his mind. He tossed his pick down and clapped both hands to his head, clenching hard fingers into his skull as he staggered around.

"Long ago and far away. Long ago and far away. Gone and forgotten. You are not that man. You are not that man."

He repeated the mantra, over and over, until his tongue thickened in his throat and the freight train hurtling round and round in his brain braked and slowed.

Heath tracked his pick to where he had tossed it. Pulled it out of a clump of prairie grass and heaved and stabbed into the riverbank, wielding the pick double-handed, alternating shoulders, like an ambidextrous demon from hell on stimulants. Digging and tearing at the earth, until sweat dripped from his hairline and coated his body, and his mind finally found calm.

The day paled into a magical gloaming. The jagged mountain peaks caught fire from the setting sun. Birds and animals skittered around, finding their dinners and nests. After two months, he was still learning the game of this desert country, how to catch it, what was good to eat. Even the fish looked different.

Sitting on his handcrafted log chair besides his campfire, he ate fried fish, wild greens, and bread damper baked into biscuits, like the cowboys here had shown him. He picked up his punctured metal mug and examined it, a laugh curling in his mind. He filled it half full of tea and whiskey, up to the mangled hole. At least she'd shot it near the rim.

Blast it. That was a bad one today. As soon as he let emotion in, let a trickle of feeling, a tiny glimmer of hope come, the memories and grief came too. There they lurked, waiting, in a dark, enclosed corner of his brain, like a monster, to grab him and drive him crazy.

It was a strange feeling—one he was getting

horribly accustomed to—not to be able to trust his mind, his reactions, his feelings. Not to be in complete control.

Not to know when it would hit.

Once that black chasm formed in his brain, the shockwaves created a network of tiny cracks, and the least thing could set them off again. And the fear was bad too—the fear of when it would come, when he'd lose control, when he'd feel that wracking pain...

He knew what healed him. Peace and quiet, open space, well away from other humans.

A Wild West frontier town suited perfectly.

Until that sparky, gunslinging, gorgeous playwright stepped off the train into town. Playwright. He shuddered.

Picnic! What was he thinking?

He had to keep his head down. Work this land for five years, and then he'd earn the land grant.

A place to rest his weary bloody bones and fried brain.

Somewhere he could stop running.

****

Opal Calahan scribbled madly in her notebook. New page, new story, how she loved it!

Stage left: Maryann rushes in and delivers a ringing slap on Oakley's cheek: Two-timing scoundrel! I'll never forgive you!

Background: Saloon bar. Gun-toting cowboys catcall and jeer.

Wait a second. That shouting wasn't her imaginary characters. Actual, real-life yelling rippled from the street outside her window.

"It's the marshal, clear the street!"

"Better git runnin', rustlers!"

In a sudden ominous, echoing silence, a horse's steady clop-clopping rang like gunshots.

She jumped up from her desk and pushed the sash window higher, letting in a blast of hot air.

A now-silent crowd surrounded a tall, sun-dried, whipcord-thin man on horseback. He wore a black leather vest, black bandana, dark woolen pants, and knee-high black riding boots. Gun belt carrying extra ammunition, two Colt six-shooters, and a coil of rope. She leaned farther out. A Sharps rifle was strapped in a diagonal holster across his chest and back. That rifle was a single-shot, full-bore rifle, .50-70 or .45-70 ammunition, powerful and highly accurate. Excellent for hunting large animals or sniping human targets.

A drooping black moustache hung nearly to the silver US Marshal badge gleaming on his vest.

Chilly foreboding shivered down Opal's spine—and not from the hotel ghosts.

A sibilant whisper went up from the street crowd, growing in strength, gathering sticks and prickles and momentum, like a summer whirly.

"Adder Jackson, the famous federal marshal is here."

A woman with downturned lips and a helmet of stiff curls shrilled, "Hunting a murderer!"

Opal stared down at the creased-in crown of his black ten-gallon hat. Adder Jackson must have felt her gaze. He snapped his head upward. Mean eyes, as though permanently squinting into the sun under his hat brim, met hers in a blaze of intelligence.

Opal ducked below the window sill, heart pounding and drumming in her chest, red blood beating in her brain. As though he'd winged her in a quick draw.

Silly. What's it to you? You're no criminal. Slowly, she rose. Forced herself to peek out again.

Those dead-alive snake eyes cut right through her, skinning her for all her secrets. For a frozen moment, Opal was utterly paralyzed with cold fear.

Something pinged in her brain. Floated away as she tried to grab hold.

She inhaled, summoned her courage, and a smile. "Good day, sir." A little shake in her voice, but not a bad effort.

Without changing his expression, he tipped his hat to her. Rode on, as slow and inevitable as winter.

Opal collapsed as though she had been released from an iron hand. What a sinister man. She pitied the poor criminal he hunted.

And then real terror shook her—the sheriff's words earlier flashed in her agitated mind—the prospector. A wanted man. Price on his head. Wanted for claim jumping. Bushranging. Murder.

She had to warn Heath.

Could she beat Federal Marshal Adder Jackson out to the prospector's camp?

She would have to stall him. Invent a tale. Send him on a wild goose chase in a different direction—for tales were her stock in trade. Her bright talent.

Opal rose and paced the confines of her room, her stomach squishing, acid burning her throat. She picked up her pen and squeezed it hard in her fist. Nothing was coming!

And if Adder Jackson got angry when he found she'd steered him wrong? Which he would. She swallowed against a dry throat.

She'd invent another tale.

Opal shoved her purse into one skirt pocket and her pistol into the other. She flung open the door, urgency clanging in her mind like a shouting crowd.

Three steps down—and she froze.

What if all the charges were true? Murderer...

Heath Rawdon was innocent. Somehow, in every cell of her body, she was dead certain of it.

Or was she?

Her fertile brain always wove stories. Had she knitted another wild tale featuring a handsome, mysterious, dark-eyed stranger, who stirred her blood to singing in her veins and called vivid life into her body? Had she invented a smoky mirror-man who bore no resemblance to cool reality?

Look at the Buck Standish embarrassment. A red flush coursed hot from her stinging cheeks over the skin of her chest, back, and belly.

She took two steps back to her room.

Blast it all to hell. Heath needed her help. She trusted him. *She fancied him.*

Nobody knew how a story would end. A strong heroine took decisive action and owned her story, for better or worse. A heroine *chose*. A heroine *fought.*

She had landed in a town called Wylder.

Opal chose the wilder ride.

She chose Heath.

Chapter Three

The marshal sucked all the air from the hot dusty street. The sight of him set her blood skittering and jumping and her brain urging her to dive for cover.

"*Hasty!*" said her brothers' voices. She shrugged them off.

"S-Sir!" She could do better than that quavering bleat.

"Marshal!" she hollered. The crowd parted as she pushed through. The shrill woman with the curl helmet uttered a protest and attempted to bar her way. Opal grinned and shouldered away the woman's outstretched arm, ignoring the affronted tones battering her back.

The federal man pulled up his horse.

Ew. That black shark-stare gleamed from the shadows of his wide-brimmed hat. It slashed into her, filleting her alive. Her verve depleted, bleeding from a thousand cuts, her skeleton exposed. The man's thin lips under the pendulous black moustache twisted as he waited. A peculiar sour, rusted-metal smell oozed from him.

She gulped. She pushed out the words, willing the tremors from her limbs. "Sheriff said he was hunting that mountain loner. I met him earlier. He walked me to town. Then he jumped a stagecoach heading east back to Cheyenne."

That suspicious stare carved into her quivering

flesh. His slender nostrils flared.

Too hasty. What if there was no stagecoach? She dug her nails into her palms behind her back.

At last, the marshal's words came creaky as a rusted gate in the wind. "Thank you, miss…?"

Damn and blast. She hardly wanted to tell him her name. No choice. "Miss Opal will do fine. Thank you, Marshal. Can't have dangerous murderers lurking around town."

She marched away, thankful that her ankle-length skirts hid her quaking knees and panic-wobbly gait.

****

Heath brushed the rich pastry crumbs from his vest and moleskins. Swished a tongue around his mouth, savoring the last taste of warm meat and butter pastry. "Best pies I've ever eaten. Thank you, Miss Opal."

"Apple for dessert?" She proffered the rosy fruit, red as her wind-whipped cheeks, shiny as her bright sea eyes and lustrous hair.

His fingers brushed hers as he grasped it. His nostrils flared as he repressed a grin. "Like Adam when he took the apple. No hesitation here."

Her lovely opal eyes flashed. She snorted. Her sweet lips made luscious shapes as she retorted, "Look around you. It's pretty far from Eden out here in Wylder."

"That's true. But it's a kind of paradise to me. Space. Silence. Big sky."

He declined the non-whiskey-spiked tea with a smile and accepted another ginger beer, so cool and fizzing in his throat. His entire frame relaxed in a contented sigh, although he could not completely collapse all his wary alertness. Not when he sat less than three yards from such a stunning example of feisty, bright, taunting, perfect womanhood.

Like being within another two strikes of a seam of gold.

All his hungers stirred. Craving to touch, hold, caress. Admire. Drown in her exquisite presence, sparkling as the brightest gem.

He could bury his face in her flower and sunshine smell.

Get a grip. She'll think you a moony fool. A woman deserves to be entertained, not stared at as though she's a two-headed kangaroo.

Her ruby lips wrapped the apple. Her small white teeth crunched. She swallowed. "Have you always been a prospector? Back home? Is it very different here?"

Home. His body froze. His brain seized. He rose and began brushing down their picnic rug, tumbling plates back into the basket, making space, moving away.

He had a backstory all ready.

But he didn't want to lie to this brave woman.

He'd spent so long repressing the truth...now he was unable to utter a word of it.

Opal rose too, hovering, biting her plush bottom lip in indecision. "Moody fellow, ain't you?" She fisted her hands on her hips. "Now your strength is restored, how about you tell me some about prospecting." She narrowed her eyes. "That was the deal."

Hell, he admired her spirit. He rasped, "Women generally run screaming from my moods. You probably should too."

She leaned in, undaunted. "I apologize. I won't ask any more personal questions. It's in the nature of females, I think, to be curious about people they encounter. And a playwright? Doubly so."

Playwright. Theater. His nerves jumped. The frown gathered heavy on his face.

Her words still flowed, giving him time to collect himself, to regroup mentally. "Your accent—I want to keep hearing it, listen to the cadence and flow, absorb its music. I like you, Mister Heath Rawdon. That's all."

He coughed. "And I like you, Opal Calahan, gunslinger." He wanted to add the rest. *Playwright.* His mouth refused to cooperate.

She noticed. She wondered, those magical eyes pinning him, brimming with care and a tiny flare of fear.

Oh, how he hated that worry. "Opal. You have no reason to be afraid of me. I will never harm you. Never."

She smiled, clearly battling unease. "He speaks! Never harm you, said the coyote to the hare."

The laugh spilled from him. "Come then. I'll show you my claim, little hare."

Whew! Opal thought. This man was a deep one. Volatile as spring rains. He did scare her, a little, but fascinated her too. She would learn about him by whatever subtle clues he dropped. If she stood his friend, maybe he would confess what burdened him.

Murderer, shrilled the crowd's voice in her mind. *Claim jumper.*

But she owed him. He'd helped her see the future, plain as that buzzard circling high in the blue sky.

She had her hidden Derringer pocket pistol and her wits.

That would have to do.

"This area has all the signs of gold country." He stood straight, framed against the backdrop of the red desert plains and shadowed, jagged mountains. He gestured to the river. "Alluvial gold. The easiest to find and the first to go in a goldrush."

A craving hunger sang in his deep voice. Obsession blazed in his dark eyes. His tall frame almost vibrated with passion. "It never leaves you. Gold hunger."

He fixed her with a burning stare. "When you strike that yellow lode—split a seam of quartz and unveil a gnarly chunk of vibrant gold—the triumph! Elation!" His fists clenched hard and red mantled his lean bronzed cheeks. "As though the earth deliberately uncovered herself. For you alone." His nostrils flared. "She teases and entices, for months, sometimes years. Offers a gleam here, a fragment there. Always promising, taunting, drawing you on. Men go mad, you know, in search of gold. They leave their jobs, their homes, their families, and follow that gleaming lure like souls possessed. Endure any hardship. Suffer any indignity. Commit crimes in thrall to gold fever."

He jerked to a stop. "Forgive me." He wiped a hand over his forehead. "I'm not mad. Just you know, the isolation...men become more themselves out here. The edges of our personalities, worn smooth by mixing with the social world, grow ragged and sharp once more."

He blinked at her and raised surprised dark brows. "I'm completely forgetting myself with you, Opal. Are you a witch, to compel honesty from men?"

A thousand replies battled in her brain. *I can see you need to talk. How do you know you aren't mad? Tell me what ails you. Speak to me of your home, your country, your childhood. Have you got a woman somewhere? Did you have one? What broke your heart?*

She didn't want to break this spell. "Show me," she said. "Show me the river, the gold, how you get it out."

He studied her. "Top secret, you understand, Opal Calahan? Word gets out, there'll be a crowd here in twenty-four hours, a new town growing on the edge of Wylder in forty-eight, and by day seven, the sheriff will have to build fifty new jails to hold all the outlaws, robbers, hard men, mining dudes, wealthy prats, drunks, hipsters, blowsies, scarlet angels, cowboys and charlatans!"

Her lips parted and her heart thrummed in her chest. "Sounds seven kinds of thrilling, though!" He grinned down at her. She added, "And Wylder will definitely need a new playhouse!"

There it was again. His face blanked. His mouth flattened. His smile flipped into a brooding, glowering frown.

Something about playhouses then.

"Of course! My lips are sealed," she said hurriedly. "How do you actually get the gold out? Hoeing in randomly with your pick there? Heath?"

As she'd hoped, calling his name pulled his attention back from whatever past hellhole he kept falling in. Appeal to specific strategy kindled his professional pride. Woke him to the present.

"Come." He beckoned with those long, tanned fingers. She came.

She followed him to his campsite, orderly and clean. A modest, tall-pitched canvas tent flapped in the nigh-permanent desert breeze. Logs were stacked neatly

31

under an improvised shelter. Brushwood chairs surrounded a fire pit dug in the sand, black with cold ashes, cleared for yards around of any vegetation, like a man concerned with wildfire sparking and spreading.

A mesh cupboard contained foodstuffs. A tub on a high stand was ornamented with a dish of soap and tiny mirror and hung with a towel.

A metal plate, bowl, and single mug with a mangled hole—guilt pinged and a giggle tangled in her throat—were stacked on a stump.

He untied the flaps of his tent and ducked inside. Emerged holding a tiny glass cylinder which glittered and glowed in the sun. "Here. A few flakes. Please accept this gift, Miss Opal, a little gold for the sunshine you brought me today. In memory of our picnic."

She held the clear tube, staring in wonder. Scattered flakes, a third the size of her smallest fingernail, floated in water. She shook the flask, and the sun picked luscious golden gleams from the gold. It drew her; she felt the lure, the spell that gold could cast.

His words penetrated her dazzled mind. *In memory of our picnic.* She jerked her gaze up at him. "You say that as though this is to be our last."

His cheeks hollowed. He looked away to the mountains cutting the skyline. His throat bobbed as he swallowed.

She tried for levity. "Wait until Buck—or worse, Cissy—discovers you didn't like their pies!"

A reluctant laugh escaped him. Dark eyes glinted at her. "You are good for me, Miss Opal Calahan. You pluck me from my moods. Now, I'll show you how to pan for gold. You'll enjoy that."

He took a stride, turned back to her. "Back where

I'm from, every kid loves panning for gold. We learn it before we learn our letters."

There! A clue! Now, a little more, and a little more. And she would be unwrapping the many layers of mystery that made Heath Rawdon, loner and prospector.

Opal hoiked up her skirts, uncaring. She half kneeled in the cold water on the edge of the river, holding the metal dish with mesh bottom in her two hands. Her knee pressed into wet mud and sharp grit.

"That's it, give it a swirl. Exactly so! You're a natural, Miss Opal. Here, see how the gold specks are heavier than the other grits and pebbles? You swirl your dish so the water and lighter grits swish away. And look what you are left with—flecks of gold!"

Opal stared open mouthed in wonder. Gold! Money! Right here in the river. For the taking.

Heath swirled the gold-studded water into another glass tube he pulled from his pocket and presented it to her. "The flecks aren't worth much." His gravel voice rasped like he'd inhaled the grit of the river bed. "Just pretty."

He handed her the spade. She hefted its weight in her arms, awkwardly dug another shovelful of gravel from the river bottom and slid it into her gold pan. She swirled—but no luck this time. A tiny pulse of gold fever gripped her. "How do you find the nuggets?"

"The river spitting out flecks like this tells us there could be decent gold either in the riverbed, in its banks, or lying in a deep seam somewhere nearby. Here, come and look at this—but be careful!"

Heath escorted her to an area piled with tall heaps of earth, stones, and gravel. Beside the mounds, a deep square pit descended deep into the ground. A pulley system made from a sturdy tree trunk and ropes extended down into the hole.

Heath held her arm while she bent over the mine shaft, peering inside, deeply fascinated. "How do you get down? And isn't it dark? and wet?"

He smiled at her. "Look at the sides. I've got a wooden ladder fixed to the sides, and I tie myself to the beam above. Most of the time. And I wear a headlamp—a small metal oil lamp attached to a special cap."

"What if the lamp goes out?" Horror coursed through her veins. Imagine being stuck in a deep, damp mineshaft, with no light. Imagine if the ladder broke, or someone removed it...*Claim jumping. Murder.*

He chuckled. "Yes, sometimes it does. Then I have to look up and hope to see the sky—sun or stars—and climb out. Hard to extract gold if you can't see."

Determination surged through her. "Can I go down there? I want to feel what it's like. Imagine I'm a gold miner..."

"It's not safe, Opal. I'm a hard man, a waste of space. It doesn't matter what happens to me. But you are a rare and exquisite flower of the desert—"

"Pish and nonsense! I've got three brothers and joined nearly all their activities, beating them in half of them too!"

Half of his mouth crinkled. "Hel—*crikey*. How can I refuse you anything?"

She stood obediently, her heart beating a rapid tattoo as he tied a stout rope around her waist. He stood so close! She felt enveloped in his strength, his clean desert smell of fresh air and wild sage, the heat pouring from his sturdy muscles. He placed a soft cap on her head, attached a small metal lamp and lit the wick.

He held her as she lowered herself toward the ladder, barely more than footholds made from split branches hammered across the smooth sides of the mineshaft. She clung to each plank, feeling with her toes for the next rung below, and the next.

The light reduced to a bright square above, roiling darkness below. The lamp flickered on damp walls, shining where the gleam of lamplight hit it, as though the mineshaft exhaled.

She hesitated, reaching with her foot, testing the walls for the next foothold. She began to shake. She was so closed in, suspended in the near-darkness with who knew how long a drop far below.

She closed her eyes and instantly lost all sense of balance. She snapped them open and clung to the makeshift ladder.

"Everything fine down there?" asked Heath's voice. "Want to come back up? I'll pull you up by the rope."

She tried to speak. Her voice came as a squeak. Tried again. "A little more! I want to see the gold." Two more steps down. Three.

"Tug on the rope when you want to come up."

She splashed down suddenly onto the damp bottom, awash with at least three inches of water. Cold water immediately seeped into her boots, clinging like icy fingers to her rapidly freezing toes.

A narrow black man-hacked cavern opened off to one side. Heath must have to crawl or bend double to enter. She crouched, impatiently pulling her mud-soaked skirts out of the way. She peered in, her brain shrieking, *No, no! Don't go into the dark.*

She crept forward on hands and knees. And then she stood up in a magical wonderland. In the darkness, her lamp picked out multicolored rocks and rich layered soils. The air smelled cool and rich with minerals. Two large, unlit lanterns nestled on a rock ledge.

A clatter in the mine shaft and flickering lamplight heralded Heath's arrival. The cavern entrance darkened as he squeezed in. Welcome body heat radiated into the short tunnel.

They bunched together in the tiny cave, sharing air, body heat, and wonder. Opal forgot her muddy skirts and wet boots, shed discomfort. "Oh, Heath!" she breathed. "Underground is marvelous!"

He put a strong, muscular around her shoulders and squeezed her to him.

"I think I've got gold fever now," she whispered.

"I know," he said. "I know."

Heath pulled out a small knife and wedged out a tiny gleaming fragment, no larger than half her pinky nail. Presented to her with a truncated bow.

She held it in her palm, examining it in the low glow of the lamps. It shone like wishes, like desire, like hope and dreams.

"Put it in your pocket."

She scooped under her skirts for her pocket and wedged it well in, under her handkerchief and pistol.

Heath led the way out of the mine and up the ladder, turning often to assist her. They burst like corks from the mine shaft, Opal giggling and blinking under the sudden bright heat of the midday desert sun.

Heath extinguished the headlamps, glanced over her shoulder, and froze.

The silence rang with tension. Opal whipped around.

A long shadow fell over them. A tall man astride a horse was silhouetted against the curve in the track which hid the bridge into town. He sat with the same graceful balance as a gunslinger. Black vest, black riding boots, black ten-gallon hat with the creased-in crown.

The leather-faced marshal. His sour, rusted-metal odor curdled the air.

He cast Opal a steady, poison-filled glare.

His words came as cold as his demeanor. "Mr. Heath Rawdon?" He didn't wait for Heath's short nod. "You are a wanted man."

Fury possessed Opal. Just when she was getting somewhere with the mysterious prospector, the marshal arrived like black mold.

This was her fault. *She didn't warn Heath.*

She'd wanted to enjoy the day.

She'd thought the officer would be gone to Cheyenne.

"Yes," she snapped before Heath could speak. Treated the marshal to her best glare. "*Wanted by me!*"

And Heath? He cut her an astonished glance, rested his arms on his muscular thighs, and his tall frame shook in a massive belly laugh. When he could speak again, he grated, "Opal Calahan, you are utterly unique. A perfect jewel."

And then he guffawed some more.

He was too busy laughing to catch the marshal's face snapping around.

To fix on Opal.

Chapter Four

The federal marshal pinned his snake eyes on her. "Best you return to town now, Miss *Calahan*. I've got private business with this prospector."

Opal bridled, jutted her chin. "That so, Marshal? Well, it so happens I'm in the middle of a visit here."

The lawman's gaze roved over her hot face. Rested on her chest, where Opal's lace modesty edging flopped down in muddy sags, exposing a good swell of her white breasts. Took in her bedraggled dress, caked with thick, flaking mud from thigh to ankle. Oh dear. What must he think of her?

Heath stepped in front of her, blocking the flaying stare. Opal breathed for a moment in the sanctuary of his height, released from that terrifyingly impersonal inspection. Like a butterfly pinned to a card.

Then she stepped around to glare back at the lawman.

"What do you want here, Marshal?" Heath asked. He folded his arms in front of his chest, and ridged muscle popped along their lengths. His stance radiated spiky alertness. A pulse twitched in his cheek.

The man didn't move from his horse. "What brings you to Wylder, Mr. Heath Rawdon? Out here, alone in the mountains?" The marshal cut another glance at Opal. His dark snake eyes flicked around the camp and back to Heath.

She clamped her lips together to hold in the lightning storm of words gathering in her brain.

Heath flung an expansive arm around the site. His voice turned to crushed granite. "I'm a prospector, Marshal. I'd appreciate it if you'd keep that to yourself. I've staked two claims, registered right and tight, but we both know things can happen."

The officer looked as though Heath had jabbed him with a pitchfork. He literally jumped in his saddle and a brief pulse of emotion crossed those leathery features. *Greed?*

The prospector added in a grating rumble, "Stuff happens under the very nose of the law." His mouth curled. "Blind, stupid, or bribed? Either way, it's the same outcome for a man like me." His right hand hovered close to his hip.

Opal watched, her heart in her mouth.

The lawman's voice issued snakey-silky from his thin lips. "Where do you hail from, Mr. Rawdon? Have first-hand experience of *things happenin'* at a claim?" He leaned forward in his saddle. His tall horse skittered sideways a step or two.

Opal's mouth dropped open. She froze still as a piece of stage scenery, hoping like mad they'd forget she was there, flapping her ears for all she was worth. Only her wide eyes moved, to study Heath.

Heath got a *look* on his face. She made mental notes. Just so should a stage actor appear, when he was trying to be laconic, but flailed inwardly with bitter, burgeoning fury. Oh no. What secrets stalked around in those mud-caked boots?

Heath deadpanned the marshal. He frowned as though his worse fears materialized in front of him. Put both hands on his lower back, stretched. "This whole claim, if you cared to investigate the county records, is entitled the Southern Cross mine. That's where I'm from. Down Under. Australia."

"And specifically?"

"Specifically, I'm from a goldrush town called Ballarat, way down south. A couple days' travel west of Melbourne town, currently the richest city in all the world. Mainly from all the Ballarat gold pouring into its new grand buildings, its silk-draped new-rich society women and their salons, and new mansions pushing up like mushrooms east and south of the great Yarra River."

"And why aren't you in Ballarat still, Mr. Rawdon? If there's still riches to be pulled from the earth there?"

"There's still plenty of gold in Ballarat, but the big gold companies have taken over now. The surface gold has all been mined. Now the mines penetrate deep underground. Large, sophisticated companies, sinking huge shafts and employing hundreds of workers."

He rubbed his nose with the back of his hand and stared toward the mountains. "I'm more of your loner type, Marshal. When the pubs get three stories with lace balconies and fancy shops spread like measles, when the—" He stopped. Added in a strangled tone, "—the *playhouses*—" He coughed. Inhaled, exhaled. "Flaunt their wares on every street, then I'm outta there."

There it was again. Playhouses. Choking. *Flaunt their wares.* Interesting choice of words. Demonstrating both longing and repulsion. Had the lawman noticed? Difficult to tell. His hard face did not reveal much emotion.

If only she could entice the marshal to play stage

villain in a play for Wylder, her success would be assured.

Opal! Pay attention.

And what was it with Heath Rawdon and playhouses? Her feminine curiosity was all riled up.

The federal man let his horse dance sideways for a moment. Then he fixed Heath with a sharp stare. "I hear tell there's a price on your head. Claim jumping. Men disappearing. Armed robbery. Care to explain that?"

"Rumor and gossip might be enough to convict a man in these parts, but I'd heard differently. I'd heard a man here is innocent until proven guilty." Heath gave the lawman a hard stare, nostrils flaring, chin jutting in challenge.

The marshal moved his jaw sideways. His gaze narrowed to bright splinters, lit with victory. This time, his words came so soft and insidious, Opal shivered in her skin. "We are making inquiries. And make no mistake. I never give up. If I have reason to hunt you down, Heath Rawdon, I'll be on your tail like a shadow you can never shake. We want no murderin' hog-wallowers in this county."

Heath's lips made a flat line in his face. His dark eyes were fathomless. His cheeks hollowed as he snapped, "There's nothing to tell."

The marshal and Heath did one of those compulsory man-staring, top-gun, position-jostling mutual glaring sessions.

Then Heath said in a forced tone, "Thank you for your efforts to keep Wylder safe, Marshal. Ladies like Miss Opal can buy their frocks and sleep at night without being bothered. But you're wasting your time hunting me."

More man-staring.

The lawman gritted, "And why am I wasting my time, Mr. Rawdon? You haven't said. Because you are innocent of any crime? Or because you think your crimes will never catch you up?"

"Doesn't matter what I tell you, does it, Marshal? You've got an idea in your head and you are clinging hard."

Opal decided to intervene. She knew about foolish male pride and the stupid lengths men would go to. Her three brothers were as bad. "Tell him you are innocent, Heath!"

Heath's nostrils flared. "I'd hate to deprive the officer of his entertainment."

"You won't be so full of sauce if I find reason to throw you in the county lockup, Rawdon."

The marshal tipped his hat to both of them. "Miss Calahan." He flashed a satiric gaze over her clothes again, drawing a flush from her. "You the Opal from the Wylder County Social Club? Perhaps I'll see you later."

"No," she responded, puzzled. "I'm at the Vincent House Hotel…"

But Heath pushed in front of her, clenching his fist at the lawman. For the first time, he raised his voice. "Get out of here, you miserable drongo."

Heath, no! This was not the moment for one of his mercurial mood shifts, from restrained courtesy to swift, flaming anger.

She snapped a look to the marshal. His formerly emotionless face suffused with wicked glee. He kneed his horse, turned, and galloped away in a spray of grit.

"What was that about? The Wylder Social Club?

I've seen that place."

Heath made a strangled sound like a choked laugh. "Better you don't know." He bit the words out, then stalked over to this tent and grabbed a blanket. "Here. Get yourself warm. You'd best head back to town and change into dry clothes." As he draped her in prickly tweed, he murmured, "You idiot, Heath! Taking a pretty flower like Opal down the mine."

She laughed and wrapped herself in the blanket. "But I'm no delicate bloom! I loved the mine. And what's a little mud?"

"It's enough to make the federal marshal forget his manners."

"How so? Heath, I don't understand."

"The Social Club. Girls with jewel names work there."

"And so?"

"It's a house of ill repute. Do you know what that is?"

"Not really?"

He snorted. Muttered to himself. Wiped his hand across his brow. Without looking at her, said, "A bawdy house. Where women sell their favors. Sell their bodies."

"Oh!" A thousand thoughts burst in her brain. She'd heard whispers of those places. "Poor girls! We have to save them."

Now he did swear, loud and long. "No, we don't."

"Well, perhaps they might prefer another career." She brightened. "As actresses, perhaps."

Heath's lean face, which had been closed and cold during that interesting discussion with the marshal, now glowed as though he'd swallowed a sun. He grinned his charming, lopsided, rakish grin. "Opal Calahan, I say again. You are an utterly unique woman!"

She laughed. Exaggerated a drawl. "Hey, goldminer. You ain't telling me anythin' I don't know already!"

They shared a smiling moment. Heath reached out and wrapped the blanket around her more securely. "Come on now. I'll walk you to the bridge. You can't stay in those wet, muddy clothes."

"You could loan me some of yourn?"

He choked. "I'm almost tempted, in case the marshal returns. To see his face. But no." He grinned down at her, and her heart turned over.

They strolled in silence, serenaded by the bubbling song of a lonely male sage-grouse out in the prairie. Opal was frankly glad to be heading for clean clothes; her skirts clung wetly and slapped her legs as she walked. Her toes curled as water swished in her boots.

"Must be a hard life, gold mining," she said.

"Mmm. Yep."

Well, that twig of conversation didn't bear any fruit. Like with her recalcitrant brothers, hinting was clearly a waste of breath. A direct assault might yield better results.

She said, "What's with your hatred of playhouses, anyhow?"

Yes! A direct hit. He stopped as suddenly as if he'd slammed into a wall.

"I'll watch you from here. The bridge is just there." His voice rang cold. His face set tight and hard, the shutters down.

She slanted a peep at him. "Maybe I'll check in with my namesake Opal on the way back."

Color mounted high in his sallow cheeks. His lips thinned to a white line. His eyes sparked like flint in the sun. "Suit yourself." The words were a dare, flung down to her challenge.

She tried another tack. "What's a Wild West town without a playhouse? People need theater to liven up their days."

His breath hissed in with a sharp inhale. With a flick of his fingers, he gestured her on. For a full minute, they strode together in heavy silence. Their feet crunched on the path. A breeze whickered softly in the long prairie grasses. The bridge into town loomed.

"I have no use for fiction," he grated. "Stories are lures, tales men and women tell themselves to ease a hard path. To beguile the mind."

"What's the problem with that? People need entertainment, relief, hope and dreams, do they not?"

"Dangerous nonsense. Tales make you soft. It's only safe to believe what you see before you, what you can seize in your grip. That's all."

His words hurt her, cast damage on what she valued, despised her deepest dreams.

She cast around in her brain for a suitably stabbing response.

"What's prospecting for gold then, except a fine story you tell yourself? Admit it: as you dig out there, all alone with the sky and mountains, wallowing in mud and despair, what keeps you digging? A picture in your mind, I'll bet. An image of you, finding a great golden nugget, pulling it from the ground, and holding it aloft in triumph."

She warmed to her theme, hardly noticing their mutual strides getting faster. "It doesn't matter how many men have failed before you—because you won't fail. What makes a man persist against all evidence to the contrary, against all previous experience? As long as there is the tiniest hope, a story to cling to, that shining tale you tell yourself, that it will be you who is lucky. You the man who finds gold."

They reached the bridge. The river burbled its own secret tales underneath.

"We need stories," she concluded with a grand gesture. "We need that shiny hope to sustain and nurture us."

His face was thunder. Heavy black brows glowered over dark blazing eyes. "You have it entirely, completely wrong." He gestured her toward the town. "And stay away from that marshal. Lawmen can't be trusted. They use their powers for their own gain. Stand-over men, preying on the weak. I hate them all."

"That's not—"

He turned and walked rapidly away, his cowboy boots clattering on the shale.

"Heath, wait!"

She watched his stiff-legged, furious walk until he disappeared around the curve in the track.

There must be some truth in what I said, she consoled herself. Or why would he be so cross?

Muddy and sticky and more than a little dispirited, Opal trailed back to the Vincent House Hotel, dodging the affronted stare of a purse-lipped woman, ignoring the appalled cries at her appearance from the young desk clerk, ordered warm water and fresh towels, and stumped up to her room.

When the water came steaming gently in a china jug, she gratefully stripped off her sticky, muddy dress and washed the cold and dirt from her body. The emotional hurt didn't wash so easily, but a clean dress and afternoon snack in the grand dining room helped restore her good humor.

She sipped her cup of tea—without whiskey—and considered. Well, everything so far was topsy-turvy. Secrets remained secrets. The hero was a wanted man, and the lawman might be evil. The heroine didn't know who to trust—and worse, had reason to doubt her own judgement.

Time for Act II. How could the heroine of this tale move things along? She sorted her mental list.

*Find out more about the prospector—but how?

*Write the first Wylder play.

*Identify potential local actors and actresses.

She drifted up to her room and settled herself at the tiny table below the window. She gazed out onto Wylder Street. To the left stood Cissy's bakery, scenting the town with the delicious aroma of hot pies and fresh cream cakes. A flush of embarrassment scorched her.

How did she get the Buck situation so wrong? Abbigail had praised him so much—and then Opal's nimble brain had invented an entire three-act play, with a grand marriage as a finale.

"Hoppy as a March hare," her elder brother Burnley always said. "And twice as hasty." Meaning too prone to enthusiasms, sudden passions, fads and fancies.

And her growing attraction to the prospector?

He fascinated her, compelled her, intrigued her. Every time they were close, the breath came fast in her lungs and her skin tingled. That man was too *present*, too hard, too wounded and secret to be merely one of her enthusiasms.

But did she see his darker side? Did she turn his flaws into fascinating mysteries?

She cut that thought away and turned her face to the right. That view was worse than the bakery! The jail and imposing sheriff's office loomed. What did the marshal and sheriff know about Heath? Curiosity spiked in her veins. At least she'd be able to see the miner if he was arrested and dragged there...

Strange how the marshal said her name. Opal *Calahan*. And the dread way he looked at her! As if he'd be as glad to put a shot in her belly as say good morning.

Craning her head farther, she spotted the Wylder newspaper office. Hmm. Reporters might have copy about strangers in town. They had all sorts of ways. She could make friends, and the newspaper could advertise her first play.

Opal pulled out her pens and notebooks. She opened to a new page. *The Gunslinger and the Rose: A Wild West Romance.*

Her pen stilled.

Why would a man fear and despise the playhouse? Had he lost a love to the theater? Had he fallen for an actress who rejected him? Did he just hate stories, deep in his bones?

No. Every human needed stories, especially in a wild frontier town like this. She would prove it to him.

Her pen bounced on the desk. She skipped from the room and down the stairs, arriving at the desk in a flurry of frills.

"Where's the local theater, James?"

"Ain't none, Miss Calahan. Plenty of bars and saloons. There's an outdoor area folks sometimes make a play in."

She clapped her hands. "We'll have to see about that!"

She'd pen another scene—and then go out into the town and find her new theater.

In her mind's eye, there it was, all gleaming and lit up in colored lights:

The Wylder Playhouse

Chapter Five

He hated lawmen. Corrupt to a man—greedy, lazy, and stupid. And that Adder Jackson—lower than a snake's belly. All Heath's hard-won internal warning systems pinged. The way those devilish eyes traveled over Opal's muddy cleavage…Maybe he couldn't blame the man. She'd been bursting from her dress, all soft and creamy and enticing.

And lucky the marshal arrived when he did. All Heath's resolutions to be alone, to keep a low profile, to find gold or make his five years working the land to get his land grant, were crumbling against the feminine assault by the glorious Miss Opal Calahan.

Heath dropped his pick and wiped his sweaty, gritty forehead. He trickled cool water down his throat from his flask. Curse it all.

If those fell Ballarat rumors caught him here…He had run from the other side of the world to get here, seeking only safety and peace. Now it might all explode in his face. Again.

He was damned tired of running.

He'd best warn the lovely Opal Calahan not to come anywhere near him. He was no man for that magnificent woman. She deserved a bright future, a safe one, after her pernicious upbringing.

A spark flashing in the distance pulled him from his musing. He raised a hand to his eyes, squinting into the dazzling sunlight. The marshal's silhouette and way of sitting a horse was weaving into the mountain foothills.

Wariness gripped Heath's lower spine.

That flash could have come from only two pieces of that black-clad lawman. His silver star. Or his gun.

Now what was the tinhorn up to?

Heath recommenced digging into the bank, checking for alluvial gold. Gold fever tugged at his senses, warring with curiosity. The tang of a wrong note about the federal man's posture clanged in his brain.

He straightened, both hands rubbing out the stiffness in his back and shoulders. He narrowed his eyes against the bright bleaching sun, tracking the marshal's headway into the mountains. He wiped and stacked his tools neatly, and went to saddle Blue, his red roan. The name was his little piece of Aussie humor, to remind him of home, where irony dictated that redheads be affectionately called "Blue." The horse would enjoy a canter out to the foothills.

He strapped on his canteen and his Colt six-shooters and nudged Blue along the line of stunted desert trees, to obscure his line of travel and suck up the dust kicked up by hard hooves.

In the distance, the marshal rode along the foothills trail and zigzagged up to the first ridge. Heath tracked him slowly, taking a diagonal approach to convey the idea that his pursuit was accidental.

The shadow scaled a crest and disappeared into a narrow canyon. Heath pulled on the reins, considering his options. The track narrowed there between two high ridges—classic ambush territory.

He trotted farther toward the mountains, taking his time.

The lawman failed to reappear, so Heath rode up the ridge, pausing at the entrance to the long dark canyon that split the mountain into a series of caves.

He didn't like the marshal looking through there. Heath had planned to hide out here himself if things ever got too hot for him in Wylder and he needed to lie low for a time before fleeing again. He had bedding and food stored in a large, airy back cave, wood stacked up, and spare tools and rope secreted in crevices in the dark rear of the cave.

The canyon led to a farther track over the mountains, which eventually led to Idaho.

Heath dismounted and squatted at the edge of the deep canyon, listening. The mountain wind sighed through the caves and canyon. No birds shrieked in alarm. A lone buzzard circled high overhead—or maybe it was a vulture. Wait. Did a horse's hoofbeat click against stone, not so far away? Rocks slid and clattered, echoing through the canyon.

Then silence.

Heath waited some more and finally nudged Blue into the narrow, high pass, blinking in the sudden dim light, shivering as cold bit his bones. He edged along the trail. No trace showed of the lawman except a stray hoofprint here and there. He looked up and around. He could spot no shapes silhouetted sharply against the tall ridges that didn't belong.

He struggled with the notion of checking his hideout cave—decided against, in case the hidden marshal watched him.

Skin prickling between his shoulder blades, he

turned Blue and trotted back to his claim, thoughts rattling in his brain like stones down a mountain. What was the trap doing? What if he found Heath's hideaway? Was this the first step to hounding him out of town?

He shuddered. He couldn't face that again. Maybe best to leave now. Find somewhere more isolated, rougher, harsher. Find a place filled with hard men who wouldn't ask questions, rather than blooming with vivid flowers of the desert like the luscious Miss Opal Calahan.

Heath stopped at the edge of his claim, sniffed the air, and assessed his camp. No new threats had materialized. He brushed and fed Blue and grabbed his prospecting tools.

He smashed the pick into the river bank. This was the problem with the demons that cursed him. At times, he couldn't trust his own thoughts. Was he inventing a huge tale that blew out of all reason, like a mad overblown tumbleweed, full of fear and panic and old, bitter failure?

He dug hard and fast, until his shoulders screamed and his stomach muscles burned and the whirling thoughts dulled back into the hidden darkness of his mind.

****

Opal slammed her notebook shut and paced her hotel room. Sass and pep sizzled under her skin and jumped in her muscles. No way could she sit still and write! Well, maybe she could create a play from what was out there, instead of dreaming up stories from inside her head. Research! Location. Characters. Time to identify a suitable building for her fabulous new

Wylder Playhouse.

She gulped the last of her tepid tea, smoothed her hair back into a chignon, and clattered down the hotel stairs. She nodded to the doorman and burst from the Vincent like a bullet from her Derringer.

Her feet began to point toward the bridge out of town and Heath Rawdon—*Hold up, girl!* Stick to the town.

She half skipped and danced along Wylder Street, unable to walk more sedately, and had almost arrived at Buckboard Alley when shrill shouting assaulted her ears. She hurried around the corner and stopped.

The woman with the sour mouth and tight helmet of curls emerged from a tall building, harsh words pouring like an evil torrent from those saggy lips. "Good for nothing! Useless baggage! Well, perhaps the whorehouse will have you."

She tugged a skinny girl in a ratty dress by the ear out onto the street and began hauling her in the direction of the train depot and the Wylder County Social Club.

The girl wept and begged, struggling against those pinching fingers. "Ma'am, I'm sorry. 'Twas an accident, I'll work extra to make it up. Please, marm. My family are counting on me for the money."

Helmet woman wrenched the girl high with one hand and slapped her hard with the other. Opal jumped. She felt that from here. The girl shrieked.

The woman shoved the girl bodily into the Social Club front garden. "You'll earn more there to pay me back. Else I'll have you arrested for theft and willful damage." The girl landed hard on the neat gravel path, tears brimming and mouth working as she stared back up her tormentor.

Outrage ignited in Opal like a spark to gunpowder. She rushed to the commotion. Opal burst into the whorehouse grounds, barely indulging her curiosity— she was too concerned for the shaking, sobbing, pleading young woman. She hoisted her from the path, brushed down the front of her patched, stained dress, and cradled the thin frame against her shoulder.

She traded snapping glares with the tyrant. "Can't be bad as all that, surely? Whatever she's done? She can hardly be fifteen—barely past childhood."

"Seventeen," the girl corrected in a muffled voice, face buried against Opal's shoulder.

The woman's downturned mouth stretched farther hell-ward. "I took her on to do my duty, as a charity to a poor family, but she's been one disaster after another."

A pang of sympathy pierced Opal for the skinny girl shaking in her arms. She knew what it was like to cause strange and wonderful accidents, from hastiness and enthusiasm, rather than evil intent.

Helmet Hair continued in outraged tones, "She said she knew how to iron and burnt the best lace cloth!"

"Never had no lace cloths in our house," the girl muttered.

"And just now, the careless wanton smashed my prize vase to smithereens! That vase came out here with my grandmother. Where I'll get another like it in this devil-infested backwoods I don't know."

The door to the Wylder County Social Club opened. A waft of perfume shimmied in the air. A gorgeously attired creature—her companion from the train!—asked, "What's all the to-do? Our girls need their rest!"

Helmet woman turned bright pink and swelled up like a balloon. "Well!" she stuttered. "Well! Addressing me directly!" She half turned, then swiveled back on her heel. Jerked a thumb at the skinny girl. "Take her. Bluebell owes me money. She can work it off in your house."

Drawing all her body parts in as though afraid of catching a disease, the shrew sneered at Opal, button-brown eyes flashing hatred. "And you—you're no better than you should be, neither." The dreadful woman stamped off in a cloud of virtuous chagrin.

The belle in the doorway smiled at Opal. "Hello, you! Coming in then, my lovelies?"

Opal grinned back. "I will one day. I'd love to have a chat, but right now I'll take this poor creature back to my hotel. She looks like she needs a good feed."

"Any time." The young woman waved an elegant hand as a large man reached from behind her and closed the door.

Opal and Bluebell regarded each other.

Hasty, said her brother Burnley's voice. Opal shrugged her shoulders. She couldn't *not* help the poor thing.

The girl wiped her snotty nose on her sleeve. "Thanks, miss. But I think I better do as she says. Go in there and earn the money to pay Mrs. Andrews for the smashed vase. And all the other things I've wrecked, broken, ruined, and cracked." Desperation shone in Bluebell's bright blue eyes. "How else can I pay her back?"

"Are you sure you have to? Maybe they were just unfortunate accidents. Working as her maid, were you?" Opal twitched her nose. The miasma of sour sweat and grime embedded in the girl's thin dress now clung to her own.

"Yes, miss. Got seven younger brothers and sisters at home. Need to send the money regular or they'll get evicted."

A Brilliant Plan came bubbling and singing straight into Opal's brain.

"You can choose to work in the Social Club, if you want. Know what they do in there, do you? Probably would make better money there than working as a nasty old woman's maid."

Bluebell's mouth creased.

Opal added quickly, "Or, not to worry, I have a Plan!"

"Plan, miss?" Hope shone afresh in those celestial eyes. Arched brows rose eagerly.

"Would you like to be my assistant?" Opal invented rapidly. "I am a playwright. I intend to write a fabulous, wonderful, exciting drama and stage it for all of Wylder and beyond. I need a main actress, stage hand, character part players—"

"Yes, miss!" the girl cut in breathlessly.

"Which role appeals? Secretary, acting lead, stage manager, drinks girl…?"

"All of them! Thank you, miss."

Opal laughed. Spat on her hand, held it out. Bluebell spat in hers. They shook hands, leaning in, smiling into each other's eyes. Opal whisked the skinny, ragged girl back up Buckboard Alley to the Vincent House Hotel.

Now, it was urgent. Her slim funds would only last so long. And with two of them?

If she didn't put on a play *and make money* from it, they'd *both* be working at Wylder County Social Club.

No doubt smashing vases and acting hastily in there too. No doubt getting the sack from the whorehouse too. The thought made Opal laugh out loud.

Time to bite the bullet and find out what she was made of.

She'd made promises now, to herself and to Bluebell.

And she still had to save her little brother Neddy from certain injury or death in the gunfighter life.

****

Bluebell wolfed down a meal fit for a wagon driver, sighed with bliss, and leaned back. "Oh, Lordy, that was like twenty Christmases come all at once." She rubbed her tiny stomach. Curling black lashes drooped over dark circles smudging pale skin. Her jaw cracked in a huge yawn. She clapped a hand over her mouth, sky-blue eyes wide and panicky. "Excuse me for yawning, Miss Opal. I'm so grateful to you! What job do you have for me first?"

Opal laughed and tousled Bluebell's silky hair. "Seems to me like you've had a long, tough haul lately. Why don't you rest in my bed for a few hours?"

Bluebell's pink mouth formed an "O" of surprise. Fat tears swam in those cobalt eyes. "Miss, it feels like so long since I rested." Her voice dropped to a whisper. "My ma, she's always fighting eviction. There's a lawman keeps on her, demanding…favors…" She scrubbed her wet cheeks with a grubby hand. "She cain't do nothin, because he's the Law. When he started setting hot eyes on me, she sent me away to work."

Bluebell hiccupped. "I gotta send her monies, else I dunno what's gonna happen to us all. And there's my next sister, Daffodil. My ma wants to keep her safe too from that wicked lawman…I miss them all."

Opal grabbed the tear-streaked girl and held her tight in a hug. "It will all work out, you'll see. Two brave, strong, capable women like us? Ha!" She released Bluebell and clicked her fingers. "It'll be a snap!"

She handed her new assistant a linen handkerchief. The girl's eyes widened in trepidation. "It's very white and dainty. Not for an ordinary filly like me."

"Nonsense! We all deserve comforts. Blow your nose now." She patted the thinly clad shoulder. "Now don't worry at all. Come up to my room now, and rest your bones."

The girl skipped eagerly after Opal as they ascended the Vincent's back staircase. In the room, Bluebell stared around, her eyes glowing with wonder and desire as she surveyed the high bed covered in its white candlewick coverlet.

Opal said, "I'll be quietly scribbling here for a bit, and then I've some errands. Order what you want. Go for a walk, whatever you like. I'll see you back here by sundown."

"Miss Opal. Thank you! No one has ever—"

"That's quite enough, Bluebell. You're just tired— you'll be more the thing once you've had a rest. Oh good! Here's the hipbath I ordered. Pull that little screen across, that's right. Make sure you wash all over now."

Bluebell's bright expression clouded. "All over, miss? Won't I catch the ague?"

Opal grinned. "You work with me, you'll be washing every day and bathing every few days. Come on now, hop to it."

A large splash heralded Bluebell's plunge into the bath. Water tinkling and plishing indicated a reasonable level of enjoyment, or at least cooperation.

Opal peered from the hotel window into Wylder Street. Hmm. The newspaper office. That gave her an idea...

She sketched out a poster that she could get printed and plaster around town.

WANTED
Actors and Folk for bit parts for New Play
Coming Soon to Wylder
Enquiries:
Miss Opal Calahan, Playwright
The Vincent House Hotel

A thought zinged in her mind like a burst of song. She snorted quietly in amusement. Then she quickly drafted a second poster.

She'd only print one of those.

Opal gathered up her broadsheets and called a cheery farewell to Bluebell. "Don't fall asleep in that bath now! Quite a pleasure, bathing, ain't it?"

"Yes, miss," answered a sleepy voice. A large splash informed Opal that Bluebell had dragged herself from the warm water. Satisfied, she pulled the door closed and scooted happily down the stairs.

Opal arranged for her prints at the newspaper office, requesting the single poster to be done first, urgent priority. Editor Daniel Martin was a sturdy, serious young man a little older than she. He raised an interested brow and efficiently began setting type.

While waiting for the single sheet, she sauntered farther east along Wylder Street, dodging cowboys, hard men, and matrons, her boots clacking on the board sidewalk. Everyone flattened themselves against nearby walls as a gilded, blue-painted surrey swept past, drawn by two white horses with plaited manes. Under the fringed canopy, a wrinkled elderly lady held a lace parasol with one hand and waved regally to the crowd with the other.

"Who is *that*?" Opal asked a nearby cowboy.

"That's Miss Delphina Mathilde Treadway, ma'am." He winked and sauntered on down the boardwalk.

Once Opal had recovered from the astonishing vision, she resumed walking—and stopped as suddenly as if she'd walked into a wall.

Right there, two buildings along from the Wylder newspaper office, stood—drumroll!

The Perfect Playhouse.

Oh my.

There she was. Magnificent. Grand. A double-story, high-roofed beauty. Sagging into her foundations a little, but that was from lack of love. Tattered latticework balconies hung askew. Once-bright paint peeled like makeup on an aging actress, long past her heyday, trying to still look the part. But underneath, she still had great bones, presence, poise.

And Opal Calahan was the woman to restore her to her rightful place in Wylder.

Behold! The future Wylder Playhouse.

Opal ran up to the building. Its lower windows

were boarded up, but she pulled two planks loose with a screech of tearing timber and squinted into the dimness inside. Ooh. As she'd hoped. A large echoing space promised plenty of room for an audience.

Ew! The room's rank breath of decaying fabric and mildew assaulted her nose, mingling with the good smells of hardwood and old wax. No matter. Easily fixed with fresh air and a good vinegar scrub.

She looked over her shoulder. No curious glances yet, but she couldn't very well climb through the window in broad daylight in the main street. Maybe around the rear?

She picked her way through mud and rubbish blown by the wind. The mansion—*her Wylder Playhouse*—was in even worse disrepair along the side. A large target had been drawn on one outer wall, and a scattering of bullet holes revealed where local lads had been doing shooting practice. Opal regarded them with an expert eye. Hmph! She'd beat them all in a gunfight here.

The rear of the building hung lower, revealing rusted water pipes and hasty repairs like an actress whose dress had been pinned roughly together at the back. Opal wrenched off more boards from a low window, wincing as the old nails screamed and protested, and peered in.

With a gulp of air to fortify her, she scrambled over the low sill, landing with a thump on a hard wooden floor below.

Darkness engulfed her. Scents of old wood, mildew, rich fabric twitched her nostrils. Gradually her vision adjusted, and she could make out shapes in the weak sunlight glimmering through the rear window.

She took a few hesitant steps, her imagination running riot. A scuttling sound froze her feet to the floor. Rats? She shivered. She peered upward. Would the ceiling fall on her? Perhaps she'd stumble over a drunk's hideaway or a thieves' den.

She took another step anyway, right hand resting on her Smith & Wesson.

A narrow back hallway opened up into a series of service rooms, kitchens, dressing rooms, and finally into an enormous, grand room. Her instincts had been right! This building had been created as some kind of playhouse or grand auditorium.

Light streaked in from the partially unboarded front windows. Pale sunbeams dancing with dust motes spotlighted a gilded cornice, a broken board on the stage, a beveled door knob, like a malfunctioning, ghostly echo of the mansion's glory days.

Frayed, bedraggled, filthy curtains hung wretchedly above a wide stage. Chairs led back into dimness, with sections gaping empty like missing teeth, where they'd obviously been removed.

Two high tiers of ornate, gilded audience seats hung above the stalls. A large recessed space before the stage offered room for an orchestra.

Glory be! Resolve hardened like steel in her heart. Here was her playhouse. Here was her future, her ticket out from the gunslinger life.

She stepped closer to the walls, peering at framed photographs and posters in thick fancy frames, hanging askew, blackened and obscured with mold and water damage. Her pulse skipped. She could just make out images of a music hall belle, a line of chorus girls, and a hero and heroine locked in passionate embrace. She would get them cleaned up.

She ran back to the newspaper office, excitement stealing her breath and spinning her heart into palpitations. The first poster was done.

She rolled it into a cylinder, accepted a box of tacks, borrowed a small hammer from the obliging newshound, and fairly galloped off through town toward the mountains.

She crossed the footbridge over the Medicine Bow River and headed west.

As she had hoped, the prospector's camp was unattended.

Giggling to herself, blood jumping in her veins, she hammered the poster to the skinny tree on the edge of the camp.

WANTED
Handsome, brooding leading man
Must have small silver knife scar on left cheek
Dark curling hair and sizzling gaze
For fabulous new play
Coming Soon to Wylder.
Enquiries, flowers,
and dance invitations
to
Miss Opal Calahan, Playwright
The Vincent House Hotel.

She snuck a quick look around. All clear. She admired her handiwork for a moment. Permitted herself a final giggle, then swished her skirts about her legs and raced back to Wylder.

On her rapid walk back, her brain fizzed with

hundreds of ideas for her drama. She adored her best idea. *Totally brilliant, Opal!*

Instead of writing the play first and then trying to discover suitable actors—potentially an impossible feat—she would write the bones of the drama, check the list of Wylder volunteers, and construct the play around them.

What could possibly go wrong?

Chapter Six

Opal didn't even make it to the bridge before a gravelly shout lassoed her, hauling her to a dead halt. "Miss Calahan. *Wait right there!*"

Her blood tingled in her veins. She looked toward Wylder town, smiling to herself. She sucked in a breath, composed her expression, and whirled.

Oh-oh. Thunder approaching.

Heath strode toward her, strong strides eating the distance, waving a white paper in his hand. The poster.

Opal assumed her most demure expression and gazed at the prospector from under her lashes. "Well, golly me. Looks like I've got a response to my advertisement already! You applying then, sir?" She looked him up and down. "I must say, you appear just about perfect for the role." She compressed her lips in a pout in case the giggles burst out.

Heath glared at her for some minutes, a muscle twitching in his scarred left cheek.

Opal smiled at encouragingly at him, blinking her lashes.

He shook the poster at her. "Would you come back for a cup of tea?" he finally rasped. "I want to talk to you."

"Certainly!"

As they walked together to the prospector's camp, she told him about Bluebell and removing her from the frightful helmet woman's clutches. Heath's brows snapped together as she talked.

He took her arm in his big warm hand. "Miss Calahan. You know nothing of this girl, apart from what she told you this day?"

"Well, she's told me a little about her family— she's the eldest, and they are always teetering on the brink of eviction—while she ate her luncheon. Starving, poor thing!"

Heath shook her arm and pulled her around to face him. "You could return to find your room ransacked and all your worldly possessions stolen."

"I don't believe—"

"You could hardly blame the child. She's in a bad way, and all that luxury might be too much for her. Or she's spun you a ripping yarn. They could be in it together, old sour-face and this girl. Haven't you heard of a quick con?"

Bitterness filled Opal. Anger flamed red in her brain. "You saying I'm too *hasty*, is that it?" She pulled away from him. "Oh no, Opal, you can't make good decisions, because you never *think*? Well, what if I just think faster than everyone? What if I've weighed all the odds and made my decision? Why isn't compassionate as good as wise?"

"Opal, Opal—" His gravel voice spiking with need hardly dented her fury.

She slapped at him. "If that girl has stolen my goods, then I'll track her down and shoot her. See? Easy. Problem solved!"

His grip on her shoulders hooked her attention to him. The urgent kiss he planted on her lips shut her up entirely.

He wrapped his warm, hard body around hers. His heart pounded strongly in his chest under her splayed fingers. His lips...warm. Tender. Seeking. The tip of his tongue licked the angel's bow at the top of her lips.

He pulled away and stared down at her with burning eyes. He rasped, "I mustn't."

With his two big, warm hands, he rubbed lightly up and down each of her arms. She found the sensation both calming and thrilling. "Come on," he said. "Back to my camp. And I'll promise not to kiss you again."

Blast! thought Opal, but trotted along with him. No way she could tear herself away just now. Her lips tingled. Her knees had gone to jelly.

The urge to be near him compelled all her senses.

****

He was dancing with fire, inviting her back. He must resist the urgent hammering in his brain, in his skin, every cell fighting to kiss her again. He could not get enough of the talented and tempestuous Miss Opal Calahan.

But he wanted to explain.

"Why...*plays*?" he asked her, by way of beginning. Coughed on the word, but he spat it out. And he was apparently still sane. She was good for him—anchored him somehow, though she was so flighty herself.

She smiled at him, that bewitching, elvish, mischievous grin that made his heart turn over every time. Made him want to shout to the wide blue sky, "Opal Calahan, be mine, from this today and forever!"

Her face sobered, and a sad expression flitted over her entrancing features. The fight sparked in his veins. If someone had hurt this lovely woman!

"I told you I'm a gunslinger. From a famous

68

gunslinger family. Could shoot about as soon as I could walk—and I'm a better shot even than a couple of my famous gunshark brothers. We've only got Da. Ma died young. And my da, he brought us up as best he could, teaching us everything he knew." She sipped her tea. Put the cup down on the dirt next to her. "Trouble is, all he really knew himself was shootin' guns."

She licked her lips, bringing a glossy shine to that pink pout. Heath's groin pulsed. *Down*. He rose from his log seat, desperate to move around, to distract himself. He brought her some herb damper bread on his metal plate. "Plate's got no hole in it," he said, voice wry.

She laughed, then went back to her story, engrossed in it now. The words tumbled, a flooded creek in spring rains.

"My da and brothers tried to girlify me, but it just didn't work. I climbed trees in my ragged dresses, fell down hills, chased deer in the forest, and always packed a pistol in my petticoats. When I grew up some, I could shoot straighter and faster than my brothers, so they all gave up.

"But a little girl without her mam still lived inside me. I peopled tales acted out with dolls made from fabric scraps and what I could scrounge from the forest. I rocked myself to sleep every night with made-up stories. The only present Da ever gave me was my first Derringer pistols. When I'd earned them. Except for one time."

"Yes?"

"One day, when I was still a little girl, my da came home with an illustrated book of fairytales. Those bright pictures! Those pretty people. Fairies, wishes, moonbeams, forests, oceans. He'd spent hard-earned coin on a book with stories and color pictures. That book opened up magic worlds. *I fell in love.* I read it over and over, enclosed and hidden in my secret hideouts. I read it until the pages were falling out, and I carefully fixed it up again, best as I could. But that book was more than the magic inside."

She fixed those glowing opal eyes on his. "That book meant 'love.' My da had picked it out, just for me. My daddy loved me. It was a piece of his heart. I clutched that book tight and never let it go. I have it still. Stories mean hope and magic and love."

He was speechless. He swallowed, throat dry. A strange ache began deep in his chest.

She pulled off a piece of damper. "Plays are stories for everyone, and for those who never learned to read, who can't get their heads around those jiggling squiggles on the page. *Plays* are hope and magic and love."

Damn it all to hell. His throat was all choked up. Tears prickled at the back of his eyes. Chrissake!

"And you?" That soft voice could charm a stone. "What's with your hatred of playhouses?"

So she'd seen him. Seen through to his pain and tortured heart. He opened his mouth. Nothing came out.

Pain lanced his chest. A pulse began pounding in his head. The black wave tickled the edges of his mind.

He inhaled. "Fancy a ride on my roan, Blue? I want to check on a cave I've got some things stashed in. There's a pretty stream there. I can check my fishing lines."

She studied him. Nodded.

The woman was an angel. Must be all those all

brothers. Gave her a kind of tolerance. A gentle understanding.

By all the saints, she was a woman in a million.

He'd tell her his terrible story, seeing as she adored tales so much, and then she'd leave of her own accord. He wouldn't need to find the guts to say goodbye.

Because the ability to warn her off, to cast her roughly away, had dwindled to the tiniest spark in his brain. Because he was utterly swamped by shouting desire, utterly magnetized by the fascinating Miss Opal Calahan. He wanted to unpeel her, layer by slow layer.

Right here, among the desert sage.

She sat close behind him on Blue, her slender arms grasping around his waist, warm at his back, as they tacked through the desert lands, into the foothills, and up into the high trail which led to the caves.

Soft white skin on her rounded forearms. Fingernails as pink and dainty as shells. An image of those fingernails sliding over his bare thighs, gently scratching the rare soft places on his body, had him bending forward in the saddle.

"Never mind, Blue. Keep going," he murmured to the horse.

Keep your wits, man.

He paused at the entrance to the steep-sided canyon, listening to the wind and the birds. No horses whickering or kicking flints down the hillside. No men's voices. No click of a gun cocking. No scent that didn't belong.

They trotted along the dim, narrow trail. The only sign of Opal wondering where he was taking her was a quick tightening, then loosing, of her hands on his hips. No doubt she had guns packed all over her. He was the one who should worry!

She exclaimed in delight when they veered down to the right and dismounted in the hidden clearing formed by a half circle of stunted mountain pines clinging to a flat ledge of bare soil. A tiny waterfall trickled into a shallow pool. Heath hitched Blue to a sapling where he could nibble sweet mountain grass and lap cool water. He pushed aside the thick tangle of buffaloberry, chokecherry, and honeysuckle hanging vertically from the ridge. He ducked under the overhang, holding the vegetation back with his forearm.

A surge of pride possessed him as Opal followed him under and stood marveling in the huge echoing space. He knew his way blindfolded in these caves, but he lit a small lantern for her comfort—and to see delight dance in her jewel eyes.

The light bounced and glittered from elongated stalactites hanging from the ceiling like carved pink and yellow spears. Humped and twisted stalagmites grew from the floor in fantastical shapes. In spots on the walls, fluorescence glowed in magical smears of greeny-blue.

"Oh! What a wonderland!" she breathed.

Heath stood tall, as buoyed up as if he had created all this with his bare hands. "Do you mind waiting here for a moment? The way beyond is slippery and dangerous. I want to check my supplies are intact. I won't be long."

"I'm coming." Her tone brooked no argument. She came.

Heath held her hand along the slipperiest sections, guiding her behind him when the path through the cave narrowed to a squeeze. He'd deliberately kept the way difficult in case of pursuit. Now, he wished he'd laid boards and nailed ropes to the walls for easier passage.

All his bedding, tools, foodstuffs, all carefully stored in boxes in cave crevasses along the way to the large rear cave appeared untouched.

The marshal hadn't uncovered his hideout. What had that lawman been up to then?

Opal shivered, dragging him from his musing. He reached out and rubbed up and down her arms, warming her. How incredibly good she felt. "Time to go. These limestone caves are cold as a stepmother's kiss. Come on, the ride back will warm you."

They cantered back through the canyon, tick-tacked down the zigzag foothills track studded with yellow pine, and rode back through red anthills to his camp.

He wrapped Opal in a blanket to ensure she hadn't taken a chill. They shared a hot drink from his one mangled tin cup.

"That's my refuge," Heath told her. "My escape route. My hideout. If they come for me, that's where I'll go."

He didn't plead with her not to tell anyone.

He trusted her to understand.

"And why," asked Opal softly, "do you need that secret hideout? Who is coming for you, Heath Rawdon? Why are they after you?"

Heath swallowed. He battled the shooting lights in his vision. Fought nausea. Clenched his fists hard and knuckled his thighs. He cleared his throat. Made a croaking noise.

Opal folded the blanket and made it into a pad. She placed it on the ground in front of Heath's chair and knelt on it, facing him. She took his hands in her own soft fingers and began to massage and rub them.

Her touch anchored him.

He forced brick-sharp words through a noose-tight throat. "I murdered my mate."

Opal's turquoise eyes widened. Her whole body stiffened. Her fingers stilled. "Go on."

He managed a tortured half smile down at her lovely face. Hell! From this angle, she was all frizzy hair, curling eyelashes, pouty pink lips, and creamy soft cleavage. He gulped and stared blindly into the desert. "Why would you care about this lost renegade?"

"I'll tell you later. Now, *go on with the story*." She squeezed his fingers hard.

The sensation brought him back to himself. He clung onto her, her touch keeping him earthed while he tried to transform into words the black, broken shapes cutting his mind.

"I hate playhouses." There. He'd said that out loud. In actual words.

"Yes, we know that! C'mon, spit it all out. Things are never as bad as you think."

That summoned a sick grin. "You reckon?"

Tell her. "My mate—" He inhaled a good deep breath of pure fine desert air laced with sagebrush and warm girl. "Me and my mate, Daniel Lonigan, struck a claim. On the Ballarat goldfields."

He stopped. Opal rose and busied herself at the campfire. She brought him a mug of tea, and he took a healthy swallow. Gave her a grin. "Whiskey-laced. Thank you."

She knelt before him again. Put her little hands around his calves. He almost groaned aloud with the pleasure of it.

"The Ballarat goldfields are a wild, rough place. Full of black sheep and desperadoes and hard men stealing identities and running cons. People from all around the great world—English lords mingling with prison riffraff, Chinese miners working with Aboriginal people, Irish rebels, and Scots engineers. All of them with gold fever. Drinking, fighting, thieving, gambling, whoring. Murdering. Taking to the hills and robbing the gold transports and stagecoaches. Bushranging."

Her eyes were alight now, glowing aquamarine. He drank another slug of whiskey-laced tea, the liquid sliding down his throat like healing fire.

"We worked that claim day and night, twenty-hour days, extracting the gold before someone tried to jump us. Almost no sleep, not enough food, filthy and exhausted. Hauling up gleaming golden nuggets— riches beyond our dreams."

Regret speared him right in the guts. "We could have stopped. We could have said, that's enough to start a new life. We could have collected the gold we had already extracted and abandoned that hellhole, Ballarat." He hit his forehead with his fist, again and again, a dull hammer belatedly knocking sense into his stupid skull.

She grabbed his fist. Held tight. Raised her arched brows at him.

The memories banged away in his head, pressing against his skull. *Voices yelling...* "The gold fever. We couldn't stop. More, more, always more in the ground. After three weeks of digging, we were skinny, hungry, exhausted, filthy creatures. We agreed; we'd take turns. One would guard the claim while the other had a wash, went into town, bought provisions, had a meal, a drink, and some company other than each other, in one of Ballarat's many pubs and alehouses. One night it was my turn."

Heath couldn't sit still any longer. Could he even keep talking? He gripped his hair and staggered off into the brush like a drunken man. The shrieking was beginning, the pain wracking him, the blackness coming—

Running steps. He collided with a soft, slender form. Sweet arms wrapped around his neck; soft round breasts pressed against him. Blood on the Cross, he could drown in that sweetness and softness.

Opal Calahan stood tough. Absorbing his need to move, to forget. "Heath. Tell me the rest. You are safe with me."

Safe. The word spread warm and seductive through his veins, better than Scots single malt.

"Walk then," he said. The movement would help. The sun was setting now. Shadows crept across the landscape. He had better escort Opal back to town before dark. But the thought was only a tiny voice in amongst the roaring in his mind.

"I cleaned myself up—how good that felt! And walked the short distance, only a couple of miles, into Ballarat town. People thronged the streets, talking and laughing, dressed in elaborate finery or miners' rough garb. Light glowed from pub windows and music spilled from the streets. And then, down the main street, the Ballarat P—p—" He coughed. Hooked Opal's arm into his as they strolled over the trackless red rocky dirt, the mint-musk scent of desert sage floating up as they brushed against it.

"The Ballarat *Playhouse* glowed like some kind of fantasy. Big colored posters lured me with beautiful women and rugged heroes, promising tales of daring and romance. I stepped up those steps into a miraculous interior, all red velvet and fringed lampshades, luxury and elegance. Full of buzz and excitement, people clad in fine fabrics. The scrape and tinkle of the orchestra tuning up—violins, wind instruments, brass. Beautiful, glamorous women. Such a contrast to the mud, hunger, and cold of our hard-scrabble, rough life. So I paid my shilling and went inside and allowed myself to be transported into a magical world."

"Yes!" said Opal. "Yes! That's exactly what it's like. What the theater is *for*. I hear nothing to alarm me so far."

Heath put his arm around her and pulled her close to his heat. As the sun went down, cold came creeping like hobyars out here in the desert.

"Tell me about the music, Heath. Was there singing and dancing?"

Vivid memories—good ones—images he had repressed deep within, burst over him. Color. Song. The whirl of the dance.

He faced her fully. Plucked her left hand and nestled it on his right shoulder, her arm resting comfortably along his upper arm. His right hand splayed firmly on her elegant back at the shoulder blade, his elbow raised and arm bent to hold her close. His left hand found her right, and they extended their arms straight out, shoulder high.

"Waltz, my lady?" he murmured in her delicate, pretty ear, her cloud of frizzy hair tickling his cheeks. He felt her nod, the quick inhale of her breath.

And then, as the sun kissed the horizon, pink and gold lighting the mountaintops in the most glorious stage scenery, desert birds calling wild music, Heath and Opal danced.

He paced rhythmically forward and back, guiding her slender shape with him, matching steps. Inhaling her closeness. Whirling her in spins and dips until she was laughing and breathless.

At last, a long gray shadow touched them where they danced.

He stared down at her, a tumult of rioting emotions searing through him. Want. Need. Protectiveness. Desire.

Regret.

Resolve.

"I better take you back, Miss Calahan. The town gossips will tear your reputation to shreds. You can't be out here after dark. You can't be out here, with me, at all! That child you rescued has likely called the sheriff or hired a cart and shifted all your worldly goods and chattels—what?"

Left hand fisted on her hip. Right hand on her pistol holster. "You finish that story, Heath Rawdon, or I swear I'll shoot a hole in your dinner plate as well. Hear me?"

An amused snort escaped him. "Opal...no." Bitterness and shame pricked in his skin. "I can't."

"You know, my da did that. He never sang the last verses of an Irish rebel song where all the rebels got killed. Only sang up to their glorious victory. I only found out when I was grown and heard the real versions elsewhere."

How did she make him laugh so often?

He couldn't bear her scorn or disdain. "C'mon. I'll walk you back safe."

"I'm not gonna go meekly back to town, and then stew all night wondering what in hell happened to make a fine man like you go so green in the gills! I'm imaginative! I'm sure I'll make up a thousand worse tales than what you are gonna tell me—right now, by the way!"

The chuckle began deep inside him, somewhere near where his hurt dwelled. Started as a small rumble, a mere vibration in his chest and guts. Hope rolled into that chuckle, and love tangled into it too, until a great tide of happiness hurtled in his blood and almost lifted him into the dark velvet sky.

Her sweet lips stretched in an answering smile.

Then her fine nostrils flared. Her eyes glittered flint in the gloaming. "My trigger finger is sure getting mighty jumpy."

Heath held both hands up in surrender.

"Listen hard then, I'll say it quick and fast while we walk." Opal's small hand slid into his. His heart jumped with happiness.

No. Time to smash Opal's attraction to him. For her sake. Walking helped. Movement always did. They neared his camp.

"I lingered too long in that alluring, magical playhouse." He swallowed against the thick wedge lodged in his throat. Held hard to her hand, anchoring him against the black tide of bitterness.

"I returned to our cold, muddy tent and claim. My mate was missing. I hunted for him around the place. Got a headlamp and lowered myself down that cold, slippery mine, in case he'd had an accident. Walked in wider and wider circles. Not a trace. No blood, no clues. Nothing."

"And your gold?'

"Gone. Almost all gone. All that gold. All those weeks of work and privation. I'd hidden a few nuggets here and there in case of robbery, bushrangers, or claim jumpers, until we could get it to the banks. That's all I had left."

"And Dan Lonigan?"

The grief hit like a sledgehammer. "My mate never returned. He was never found. He was a popular bloke. I was accused of his murder, locked up before the trial, got off as I was in the playhouse that night, but everyone always said I did it."

They were nearing the bridge into town. "People cursed me for a killer and thief wherever I went. Refused to serve me in the shops, refused to take my 'blood money.' After a year of this, getting worse every day, a whole gang of blokes I'd considered mates beat me up—again—and ran me out of town. Cursing me for a claim-jumping mate-killer."

Wylder was gearing up for the night. Warm light spilled from saloon windows, women called from the shadows, cowboys jostled each other on the board sidewalks.

"Keep talking, Heath."

"I'll take you right to your hotel. This whole place changes after dark. You need someone to look after you, Opal."

"You offering, prospector?"

He growled in his throat. Muttered, "What I'd give..."

Finish the story.

"I allowed myself to linger in that playhouse. Enjoying the show, the music and dancing a balm to my culture-starved heart. Mixed with the company there, talking of theater and books. And meanwhile—"

"You can't blame yourself!"

The familiar wave of guilt and grief smashed over him. Heath released Opal as his knees buckled and he fell heavily on the hard ground. Words jerked, his face half in the dirt. "I'm broken. They destroyed me. Once I escort you back to the hotel, you must promise to leave me be. Never come back. I've told you my fell tale."

"No! I will do nothing of the sort. Heath!"

Weariness tugged on every muscle of his body. A passive, floating unconcern possessed him, as though she'd drugged the whiskey tea. He wanted to just give up. Fade away quietly. Die.

Slap. Slap, slap, slap. "Whoa! That almost feels good." He shook his head muzzily and sat up.

Must get her home safe.

He pulled himself to his feet.

"I apologize, Miss Opal. You can see—I'm not in control of my mind. I can't be the man for you. I've committed the worst crime on the Ballarat goldfields— let down my mate. Murdered my mate. The foulest crime. I was hounded and cursed, but the voices in my head got louder than any harsh words on the street. I should never have left him for so long.

"I took a ship to America. Headed to the other side of the world. Far away. Losing myself in space and quiet and nature. So here I am."

He gazed at her lovely face, creased in horror and sorrow. For him.

He said softly, "Now, I never can bear any blasted

playhouse."

He pulled her head to rest on his shoulder, caressed her crazy hair. "And here we are at the edge of town. I'll walk behind you to your hotel. But Opal? Never come back. *I don't want to see your face again.* Don't want to hear your voice. Now walk. I'll be right behind you, seeing you safe."

She pulled away, the better to glare. Rebellion sparked from her frizzy hair to her tapping boot. Her cheeks bunched up, lips pressed together.

"Shh now," he said. "Just go."

At last, she turned and went.

He followed close behind, protecting her from danger.

Chapter Seven

The Vincent House Hotel was lit like a candelabra, windows framing glowing scenes of laughter and rich warmth. She halted in the entrance, peering out into the dusty, vibrant street. A tall, muscular form melted away into the cold, gray shadows.

She returned Parkinson's cheerful greeting as he held the door for her. She fumed inwardly as she mounted the internal stairs two at a time.

Blast the man.

Never visit him again? Wrong man for her?

He'd uttered those stinging words, despite their ride and the marvelous cave. Despite their shared laughter. He got her jokes quicker than other fellows she'd bumped against.

And he made her feel…well, for a writer, she was sure bereft of words.

She paused, one toe on the riser ahead. Her muscles melted into the memory of his body heat, as they twirled together in their strange and beautiful desert dance. Her body swayed, reliving his broad muscular form guiding her with easy grace. That gorgeous, precious moment while the mountains caught fire, and the earth held its breath, and they spun close together, in perfect harmony.

Blast him to hell and back for a stubborn, bull-headed, misguided…hero.

83

Conviction settled diamond-hard. The man was no criminal.

Well, she'd already run after him twice now. If a man was interested, he'd come chase her.

And this hard-working playwright had Things To Do. People needed her.

At her room door, she hesitated, hand held out mid-air. Was the prospector correct? Had she made another hasty misjudgment, and had Bluebell stolen every stick and stitch of possession and clothing?

A sick feeling whirled in her guts. She braced herself.

Opened the door.

"Miss Opal!" Bright blue eyes shone wide with relief. The spick-and-span room gleamed. A tray covered in a tall silver dome exuded delicious smells curling from under its rim. A fat pot of tea and two floral cups promised revival.

"I—I thought you'd be hungry, gone so long," said Bluebell piteously. "Did I do right, Miss Opal?" Her little hands twined together anxiously.

Opal rushed forward in a surge of gratitude and hugged the skinny girl to her. "You did *perfectly*, Bluebell! I'm so impressed. This is exactly right. I'm utterly starving hungry."

Bluebell stood straight, flushing rose-pink with pleasure. She marched to the small table and raised the silver dome like a show woman to reveal a plate of greens, fried chicken, vegetables, and grits. "For you, madam! And," she added triumphantly, "I paid for it outta a few coins I saved from my work at Mrs. Andrews."

"Bluebell! You are my assistant now, and you must

promise to put everything on my bill, do you hear?" She added hurriedly, as the girl's bright face fell and tears spangled the tips of her long lashes, "But this is the most wonderful, thoughtful present. Thank you." She squeezed the girl's work-worn fingers. "I accept."

Opal knew all about poverty and dignity. And how.

It was the right thing to say. Bluebell brightened immediately.

The poor child had only ordered one dinner. Opal pulled the saucer out from under a tea cup and piled a slice of cooked grits and hot food onto it. "This will be fine. I'll have the teaspoon and the knife. You have the plate and the fork."

Bluebell stared in wonder. "No, miss, that's not right."

Opal retorted, mouth half full of the warm, tasty food, "C'mon. I need a strong, feisty assistant. We've got a big day ahead tomorrow," she added, improvising wildly. "We're sharing this good food."

Bluebell gave her a shy smile lit with bright hope, giggled, and collected her half of the meal, crockery, and cutlery.

****

Next morning, after a refreshing sleep in the large, soft bed, Opal and Bluebell took turns washing at the jug and bowl.

Opal spoke to Molly Maguire, who efficiently organized a trundle bed to be placed in the women's room later that day, and good-humoredly waved away the extra for the room bill. "I saw how much that skinny child eats at breakfast this morning. No extra charge for the room—we'll make it up in all the food. And you are very welcome, my dear. We are all so excited at the prospect of a playhouse in Wylder! My, before we know it, there'll be a grand bronze plaque on the front door, proclaiming, 'Famous Playwright Miss Opal Calahan stayed here!' "

Opal giggled. "Oh, go on with your blarney, Mrs. Maguire." But a warm, excited glow suffused her all the same.

She and Bluebell collected her posters from the newspaper office and set to it, plastering wanted posters all over town seeking potential actors, actresses, stage hands, conjurors, animal tamers, and more.

Within an hour, the playwright and her assistant were trailed by a grubby stream of snotty, jostling children, yelling a cloud of questions and suggestions.

"Can we have a magician, miss?"

"...ponies what do tricks?"

"...Josie wants clowns!"

Opal beamed at the gathering throng of cowboys, fancy women, bartenders, and mine workers. "I'm seeking folk to act in my play—no experience needed. Who's up for some fun?" The horde cracked jokes and pushed each other forward, and then a show of eager hands warmed her. She scribbled quick notes of names, potential characters, and costumes.

What a brilliant idea to recruit actors first, and then create a play around them. It wouldn't take her long to write the play—the urge had been hammering and yammering at her for so long, hadn't it?

As she worked, every time she caught a whiff of leather and desert sage, she whisked around—but it was never the prospector, only cowboys, ranch hands, miners. Was that his curly dark head towering above the crowd? She'd rush over, only to be disappointed.

86

He's not coming for you, she reminded herself. For the thousandth time.

And then she'd remember the dance, how he'd held her like the most precious gem, his dark, romantic stare sizzling her right to her bones, softening her all over; and she'd begin fantasizing all over again.

So perhaps she wasn't being very selective with who she signed up for her play.

"You want actors?" A woman waved and called from across the street. "We'd love to help you out!" She hustled through the dust, wagons, and horses, hauling three toddler boys with her, parting the crowd around Opal by main force and the power of her resonant voice.

"You got incredible range, ma'am," Opal said in delight. "Perfect for my grand playhouse!"

The woman's booming tones nearly stripped Opal's ear from her head. "I'm Olive, wife of Wylder's leather tanner Nartan Sagebrush. These naughty triplets here are Winter, Moon, and Sparrow Sagebrush." The toddlers wore tiny beaded leather shirts, breechcloths, and fringed leggings.

The old saw floated through Opal's mind—*never have children or animals on stage*—but she pressed that negative idea resolutely away. She must have them! The triplets were so cute! She would write in a role for them as soon as she got back to her writing desk. She gave Olive a huge hug and kiss and said rehearsals would begin soon.

In record time, Opal had signed up the Sagebrush family, three cowboys, a luscious girl called Garnet from the Social Club, Violet Bloom the school teacher, Luke the blacksmith and his girlfriend Jilly, and sundry pistoleros, card sharps, and saloon girls.

It was happening! Excitement sizzled in the air.

Only one little problem. None of the men wanted to be the leading man. All three cowboys, Leroy, Quentin, and Driver said, "Just a walk-on part for me."

"I'll create the stage scenery," Luke the blacksmith said. "And loan you any weapons needed."

Opal and Bluebell returned to the Vincent for luncheon, fired with the success of their morning's work.

This afternoon, Opal would begin creating her Wild West romance-drama-comedy-circus-magic show. Goodness, she had promised rather a lot to people already!

****

A dark gaze drilled, smoldering with need. Then filled with raw anguish.

She flung down her pen.

Curses! She needed a different leading man bouncing around in her brain. Then the play would surely come. "Bluebell. I'm away to talk with Cissy and Buck Standish for a little. You keep making those notes of people and roles and jobs. I won't be long."

"That's what you said yesterday." Those wide innocent eyes sparkled, teasing, with a smidgen of fear.

"Bluebell, you are safe here. No one will get past the doorman Parkinson or Molly Maguire. If for some reason you feel afraid, hurry to the bakery. Cissy and Buck will see you safe." Opal rubbed the thin shoulder. "Buck wants to hear about his little sister Abbigail, who is a dear friend."

Her assistant nodded, and Opal hurried away.

She walked up and down in front of the bakery,

trying to reason herself out of the hot blush that stung her cheeks and the trembling that afflicted her limbs.

She *hadn't* embarrassed herself. She'd burst into the bakery, yes, but she *hadn't* flung herself bodily into Buck's arms and declared her passion for the gunslinger.

They didn't know, they *couldn't.*

And yet, when she pushed open the heavy door, the sweet tinkling bell sounding more like a death knell in her tingling-red ears, lovely Cissy cast her a satiric, questioning look. *What do you want with my husband this time?*

Blast it. She did know.

All that morning as she had hiked past, rushing one way and another, she'd peeped into the bakery window, waiting for a chance to go in. Never a lull. First the breakfast swarm, then as that trailed off, the mid-morning coffee rush, then that barely lessened before the early lunch mob swilled hungrily through the bakery.

Opal couldn't blame the townsfolk. It all smelled heavenly. Glorious slices of glistening cherry pie. Squidgy decorated cakes that made her mouth water.

Buck and Cissy were busy, as usual, instructing the help, carting heavy trays of buttery pies, small cakes, and tempting cookies.

And the fact slammed hard into her—a gunslinger could reform. Could change their life. Settle. If the most famous gunshark in the west could do it?

So could Opal Calahan.

The thought gave her courage. "Sorry to disturb, ma'am. I came to tell Buck about his sister Abbigail. And to maybe…" Opal quailed a little.

"What is it, sweet girl?" said Cissy in her soft voice, coming to rest a gentle palm on her shoulder. A sudden grateful tear brimmed and flowed down Opal's cheek. Gosh, the woman was gorgeous. Inside and out.

Gorgeous—and pregnant. Her apron swelled over a good-sized baby-bump.

Opal dashed the silly tear away. "Maybe you've seen the posters all over town? I'm the new Wylder playwright." She puffed her chest out. How good that sounded!

"And I...and I..." It had all sounded fine when she rehearsed it in her head! Her mouth just started talking, the words bursting in a torrent. "And I was hoping Buck Standish would consent to be my leading man. Or at least rehearse the part. But it's fine, no matter, anyone can see you are shockingly busy, sorry, I get these ideas, and then I have to act, and then there's consequences I didn't foresee—"

"Here. Have a biscuit," interjected a deep voice. A wide, strong hand plucked up hers, filling it with a yeasty biscuit studded with tiny gleaming currants.

"Lord, how delicious," Opal said and took a huge bite. Embarrassing flow of words effectively stoppered. Clever Buck.

"Here, take a seat. I'd love to hear how Abbigail is faring." He gestured to the single cute table covered in a checkered tablecloth, decorated with a tiny vase bursting with a purple wildflower. He waved away Opal's protests about taking custom away. Cissy brought her a cup of tea to go with the biscuit, and they sat either side of her, peppering her with questions, occasionally leaping up to serve customers when their bakery assistant was busy.

Lovely people. Somehow, Opal found herself telling them all about her love of the magic of plays, her belief that they can change people, her growing passionate desire to shrug off the gunslinger life. To bring her youngest brother to Wylder before he was maimed or worse. To give Bluebell gainful occupation so she could keep her family from the dreaded eviction.

"Of course we will help you, Miss Calahan," said Cissy.

Tears stung Opal's cheeks once more. "I don't how to thank you," she said. "Thank you for understanding so well."

Buck promised to act as leading man in her play, and Opal shook hands with them both in farewell. Cissy pulled her closer and engulfed her in a hug. "Follow your dreams, Opal." She held her at arms' length. "There's something else, isn't there? When you need a woman to talk to, you come to me, you hear?"

Opal changed color. Somehow, Cissy had divined her roiling, conflicted emotions about the prospector. Mad man. Wanted man.

Cissy whispered, "The best guide you'll ever find is right here."

And placed a hand on Opal's heart.

****

The best guide you'll ever find is right here.

Opal walked down Sidewinder Lane, crossed Old Cheyenne Road and the rail tracks, and let her feet take her down Sundown Lane toward the bridge over Medicine Bow River.

She wouldn't cross the bridge. Just have a little ponder. Stay here on the safe side of town.

As she reached Bone Orchard Road, she hurriedly

drew back into the cluster of buildings crowding the road where it dog-legged just there. Her heart pounded.

The best guide...

The marshal, sitting tall on his black horse, emerged from Copper Alley, facing west to the Medicine Bow Mountains. His gray afternoon shadow stretched back east toward the cemetery on the edge of town. As though he trailed death behind him.

Opal shuddered.

She pressed back into the doorway of the anonymous building as he trotted along Bone Orchard Road, right past her. A whiff of his sour, rusty smell stung her nostrils. That man sure gave her the shivers.

He stopped and peered into the shadows where she stood hidden, as though he'd sensed or heard her somehow. Opal froze. She smothered a frightened yip. She slowed everything down, just as her daddy taught her about aiming and shooting a gun—stilled breathing and muscles, calmed thoughts and emotions. She cast her eyes down, lest a glint give her away.

The black-clad lawman clip-clopped over the bridge. Opal breathed out. He headed west toward the mountains.

Toward Heath.

The lawman faced into the foothills, leaning forward now like a greyhound after the bait. She inhaled, then skittered across to the cover of the last building on the street. Phew. Bit stinky. Mingled strong scents of soapy water, mud, and the more astringent waft of human urine wafted. She waved an impatient hand in front of her nose.

She waited, heart jumping in her chest, legs prickling and tingling, ready to burst into action. She inhaled and walked into open space, her skin shrinking. Determination drilled her. She marched over the bridge.

In the distance, the marshal didn't turn around.

He was focused on his prey.

But nohow would she leave the damaged, magnificent Heath Rawdon to face that viper all alone.

Something about that marshal...a dark shape flashed in her brain, laden with terror. A long-ago scream echoed, the sound dying into a choked gurgle.

The memory-shape in her mind slid away as soon as she tried to grab hold. Gone. He reminded her of something—or someone. From way back.

She picked up her skirts and hustled along, lips firm with purpose.

The afternoon sun beat on her head under her bonnet. A damp bead of fear-sweat trickled between her breasts.

A vulture circled high in the sky, an ominous black pinprick against the blue.

Like its black-clad human echo below.

Chapter Eight

Heath registered the slow clip-clop of a heavy horse somewhere above, the ground vibrating as an unexpected visitor arrived in camp.

He stilled in a bent-over posture, his small pick hacked into the promising lead in the deep, cool side-tunnel of his claim. A wave of frustration smacked into him. Couldn't they just leave him alone? Who was it this time?

Unease replaced annoyance.

He lowered himself to his haunches so he could straighten his back in the dark, damp tunnel. Listening.

Jingle of spurs. A horse whickered. Footsteps. Nobody called out. Someone walking around his claim.

Fury mounted now, and his muscles shook with it, with the rampaging urge to climb out of his mineshaft and confront the intruder. He'd catch them in the act of whatever spying they were up to and show them he wasn't a man to mess with.

He crept silently from the side tunnel, straightened as the square of bright sunlight hit him in the face from the entrance high above. He put one hand on the guide rope, one foot on the first rung of the rough ladder hammered into the side of the mineshaft.

The entrance light darkened as a man peered down, silhouetted against the sky—Heath couldn't make out the features. But he knew the shape of that creased black ten-gallon hat.

"Hey!" he yelled. The face disappeared. A fast chopping noise.

The safety rope shivered and jumped in Heath's right hand. It slackened and fell into the mine like a dead python. Heath stared at the cut rope in dismay. "Marshal! What's your game?"

Surely the lawman knew that was a fast way to kill a man.

Now Heath would have to edge his way up the slippery sides of the mine shaft, clinging to rough planks, hoping like blazes that they held...

The square of light above him went black on one edge. The lawman was sealing the mineshaft! "Hey, Marshal! Man in the mine!"

Heath listened helplessly to the scrape and bump as the lawman dragged the cover across. Cold fear slithered along his spine.

Enough.

He picked up the muddy cut rope, tied it around his waist. He might be able to secure it in stages to the planks lining the mine as he climbed. Thank all his stars he insisted on safety—some men just had the guide rope. No ladder planks; just a couple of foot spikes. Too many things could go wrong.

'Specially of the human kind.

As he pressed one foot on a plank, a hand pushing against each side of the shaft for leverage, and searched with his boot for the next foothold up, scenarios ran through Heath's mind. The marshal, waiting silently up top, gun in his hand, ready to ping Heath the moment he emerged from the shaft.

The marshal, planning to shove Heath back down,

causing injury, impairment, or death.

He inched up the slimy walls, fingers clenching hard on rocks studding the walls, not wanting to rely totally on the rough wooden ladder.

The lawman must not have an arrest warrant. He would have just collected Heath and thrown him in the Wylder lockup. No, the man had a deeper game.

Claim jumper whispered up his skin.

A board pulled suddenly out of the shaft wall. Heath slid, scrabbling frantically for purchase. He clung with strong fingers to a thin plank. Slammed his body hard against the rough, damp mine-shaft wall, heart smashing in his ribs, blood pounding in his head. Pushed both feet hard against the opposite wall, wedging himself in the shaft.

He sucked in air, using deliberate calming breathing, like he'd learned to use to calm the crazy thoughts when they came.

Hell! A woman's voice. No, Opal! This lawman was dangerous. Unpredictable.

Raised female haranguing now. If he wasn't so imperiled, he would have laughed. Miss Calahan's voice tore into the marshal.

"Opal!" he roared from inside the mine, the sound echoing and colliding in his ears. "Get back to town, now!"

A shot rang out. *Holy mother of God.*

Fear lent Heath wings. Superhuman strength. He grabbed and pulled and jimmied himself up, up to the top of the shaft.

Listening all the while to the horrible, ringing silence.

He braced his feet on the rough ladder planks,

praying they would hold. He pushed hard at the mineshaft cover.

It shifted. Weighted down, but not fully. Opal must have come in the very nick of time.

He'd kill her for risking herself. If the black-clad marshal hadn't already...soon as he got himself out of this nightmare.

He heaved upward on the square of heavy planks, pain lancing his straining shoulder muscles. Pushed again. The cover moved across three inches. A crack of blessed daylight stabbed, sent his eyes blinking and watering. He climbed right to the top of the shaft, crushing his shoulder against the cover, pushed his fingers in the gap, and flung it away. He burst from the mineshaft and spilled out onto the dirt.

Heath leaped to his feet, crouching and looking wildly around, ready for action.

The marshal hovered three paces from the mineshaft, hands in the air, a malevolent expression darkening his saturnine features. Frozen.

Heath whipped his attention around.

Opal Calahan stood a short distance away from the mine, straight and fierce, a pistol cocked in each hand. All business.

In that precise second, Heath Rawdon fell utterly, completely, stupidly in love with her.

No going back.

The air twanged in a long beat. Opal said, her sharp gaze never leaving the marshal's face, "Y'all right there, Mr. Rawdon?"

"I'm fine. No thanks to this supposed lawman here."

Adder Jackson slowly lowered his arms, gaze fixed

on Opal's gun hands. When she made no move, he looked at Heath, his snake eyes flat and wary. A false smile creased the leathery cheeks. "Just trying to help a lone man. Thought you'd left your mine uncovered. Doin' my good deed for the day."

Heath snorted. "That's why you cut my guide rope?"

He glanced over his shoulder. He and Opal gazed at each other, in unspoken communication. Nothing they could do, except be extra vigilant. Heath might have to hire another man in town, although that came with its own extra risks.

"Don't know what you mean," said the marshal, in silky, sibilant tones. He strolled in jerky movements to his horse, grabbed the reins. He shot a mean-eyed look at Opal. "Some folks are mighty trigger happy. What are you doin' here, all on your lonesome, *Miss Calahan*? Young filly like yourself is best holed up in town with the other nice ladies."

In one smooth motion, he mounted his tall black steed. He screwed his leathery neck around and glared down at her. "What would they think now, if they know'd you venture out here constantly, visiting a man wanted in other jurisdictions? All by yerself like a floozy?"

"Leave her out of this," Heath snapped.

"Is that a threat, Marshal?" Opal whipped back. "And maybe a certain lawman's reputation would take a beating, at that, if it becomes known he tried *to kill* a lone man working a claim out here? *Questions might be asked*, Mr. Adder Jackson."

The lawman's face blanched under his dark tan.

Phew. Brave lass. Undaunted and fierce. Heath's

stupid heart did somersaults. His fists clenched ready to drag the man from his horse and punch him to blazes, if the man insulted or threatened Opal again.

The marshal's thin nostrils flared. "Perhaps we'll shroud this…misunderstanding…in mutual discretion, *Miss Calahan*."

Opal merely smirked and raised her brows. "You'll just have to wait and see, won't you, sir?" she replied sweetly.

Heath wanted to kiss her.

The sinister lawman treated Opal to a dark, frustrated glare. At last, he wheeled his horse and trotted off through the sparse prairie grass toward the foothills and the canyon path through the mountains.

Opal sat with a thump on one of Heath's log stump seats. Her eyes were wide and troubled as they met Heath's concerned gaze. "That man…he reminds me of someone. A dark shape. Maybe from childhood. He flashes in and out of my memory before I can properly grab hold." Her gaze sharpened as she took in the state of him. "Right. Get in that tent and take off those damp, muddy clothes."

"Why, Miss Calahan, I'd be delighted."

Her cheeks pinked delightfully. Then they both laughed, a little uncontrolled. She sobered. "Why does the marshal always say *Miss Calahan*, in that snaky, hissing voice? Like he knows me."

Heath sat next to her and took her hand.

Inspiration brightened her features. "Maybe he knows my brothers. Or my da. Yes, that might be it. In some circles, *Calahan* is a famous name."

"Gunslinger circles."

She nodded. "Still doesn't make a lotta sense." She

shook herself. "Come on now, get outta those muddy, wet clothes. I'll take them into town to get cleaned for you." She studied him. "A bath wouldn't go amiss on you, neither."

Heath pretended to be wounded. "What can you mean? I wash in that freezing cold creek every morning." He smiled at her. "I don't need to change clothes. I'm a miner. Mud and damp are our element. No use donning clean gear. It will just get muddy and wet again tomorrow. Besides, clean clothes don't matter when you have a face like a dropped pie."

A charming giggle danced on her sweet lips. "Won't hurt you to put on dry clothes. You've had a shock. Faced death at the hands of the law, your supposed protector."

He tried to distract her. "I've got one other set of shirt, trousers, and vest so stiff with mud you could use them for house bricks. Else I've only got my Sunday clothes."

"Oh?" Her gaze warmed. A rosy blush stained her cheeks. "Well, I might have a yen to see you all dressed up."

He couldn't resist those wide, bright opal eyes. "Walk back toward the bridge then. Stay in hollering distance in case any more twisted lawmen come by."

"Why?"

The grin escaped him. "You can stay here if you want. But I'm not putting my nice, clean, quality Sunday clothes on over this mud-caked skin. I'm peeling off my clobber on that bank there and jumping buck naked in that creek first."

"Oh!" Opal's neck and ears crimsoned. She hunched her shoulders and giggled. "Very well. I'll walk slowly to the bridge and back. By then you should be decent." She cut him a look. "Why not come back to town, book a room somewhere, and have a proper wash and meal?"

Desire pinged in his blood. For a moment, the vision danced, a shimmering mirage in the dry desert of his life…clean clothes. Dinner with Opal. Music, conversation, laughter…

Black shutters slammed shut on his brain. No. No pleasure. *Don't leave the mine*.

"Heath, what's the matter?"

He forced his lowering frown to ease. Then he loosened his tight-gripped lips and slowly relaxed his neck and shoulders. "Can't leave the mine," he snapped out, and instantly felt bad.

He summoned a lighter tone. For Opal. He arranged his features in a comic grimace, glanced over at his metal plate and bowl. "When all those gunshots were snapping around the camp, I had to rush out of that mine shaft pronto! Had a terrible fear for my dinnerware. Worried I'd find a new bullet hole decorating my remaining plate."

Opal laughed. Her whole expression glowed.

He said, before he grabbed her and kissed her, and to hell with the mud, "Go for your walk. When you see a handsome, clean stranger here on your return, don't forget to say gidday."

Opal grinned. "I won't!" She headed out on the track, turning once to send him a saucy look that sent the blood racing in his veins.

Heath raked out the ashes and set a new fire. Set a billy to boil for shaving water. Shot a glance up the track and pushed down the sudden, shocking wish that

Opal would return and tend to him. Tried not to imagine her soft hands on his body as he ripped the wet, filthy vest, shirt, and undershirt from his upper body. Tried not to see her sweet lips smiling invitingly as he pulled the clinging, muddy trousers from his form. He stalked naked to the lower reaches of the creek, below his camp, and splashed into his bathing hole. He crouched in the small rapids. Let cold water sluice his heated desire from his unworthy skin. He submerged his face and hair to drown sensual fantasies.

He cleared whiskers from his cheeks with his straight razor, trimmed the black beard along his jawline, and waxed his long dark moustache into a gallant handlebar.

By the time he unfolded his best shirt and newest moleskins, donned a fresh leather vest and dry, polished boots, he almost felt human.

Deserving of being part of the human race.

No, that can't be right!

He waited for Opal, blood skittering in his veins, nervous and excited as a new colt in a paddock. He rubbed agitated hands on his thighs, then lifted them—don't grime your new clothes, fool!

Opal appeared along the track. And the expression on her face made him feel he'd found gold at last.

Her mouth opened. Her eyes widened to summer-ocean aqua-blue and sea-emerald. The blush mounted her cheeks. Both hands shot up in the air. A smile blazed across her vivid countenance like a blessing. A valediction. Welcoming him home.

He scraped a hand through his damp, combed hair. Tugged the bottom of his vest, to check it was straight and tidy. Fought a wave of prickling shyness surging under his skin. He gazed at his boots for a moment and breathed in, hard. Raised his head to gaze back at the only woman for him.

She'd changed her dress. Checked cobalt blue, the color of an Australian summer sky. Saucy ruffles at the neckline. Tiny diagonal frills hooking his gaze to the shape of her hips and legs. She'd smoothed her frizzy cloud of hair into an elegant pompadour at the front and long gleaming brown ringlets tumbling over her shoulders and back. Tiny blue bows securing curls of hair above her ears.

A jaunty half boot protruded from the hemline frill.

His resistance crumbled to dust and blew away.

Heath stood tall and proffered an arm, proud of his crisp linen sleeve. "Miss Calahan. May I have the very great pleasure of escorting you into Wylder for dinner and conversation, followed by music and dancing?"

Opal gave him a saucy look under curling lashes. "Mr. Rawdon. That is you, all spruced up and handsome? I'd be delighted."

Handsome. His blood hurtled.

She stepped forward and lightly touched his waxed moustache. "I like this," she said softly.

His groin pulsed. "Come, then." It came out as a growl.

They walked along the desert track toward the bridge and Wylder. The sun hung lower in the sky, and the mountains had drawn on their afternoon colors: purples and pinks, bright blue and dark slate gray. A flock of birds flew in arrow formation across the sky, piping a high song. Tiny curls at Opal's hairline shivered in the herb-scented breeze. He longed to loop a fingertip in one and brush that delicate, soft skin.

"...and Buck Standish is too busy to do all the rehearsals," Opal said. "So I need a leading man to help me practice the lines. Just to get them straight, you understand? Hear how they sound, if I need to make adjustments. Perhaps inject their own fun phrases to liven it up!"

Heath had the distinct feeling he'd missed something important while staring like a love-sick koala at the tiny ringlets at her neck.

"A dilemma indeed," he answered cautiously.

They stepped over the Wylder Bridge, the Medicine Bow River rushing and gurgling beneath them, much shallower now it was early summer. Heath loved having Opal on his arm. He stood straighter. He walked proud. Something tight and frozen eased in his chest.

The first whispers tickled his neck after they'd strolled laughing up Copper Alley, crossed Old Cheyenne Road, and headed up Sidewinder Alley.

"Thief!"

He shrugged a little. The black memories tugged at the edges of his mind. He put his hand on Opal's where it rested warm on his sleeve and smiled into her lovely face. He must have misheard, that was all.

"Murderer!" A hiss from a doorway. Heath halted.

He resumed walking, picking up the pace slightly. Heading for Wylder Street, just ahead.

He relaxed as they stepped up the grand entrance steps of the Vincent House Hotel, the emotion swelling within him. Pleasure. Pride. Happiness. He tipped his hat to the doorman and ushered Opal to enter in front of him.

Now he could hardly wipe the grin plastered all

over his face.

"Heath! Stop frowning! Why are you looking so serious and stern?" Opal whispered.

His heart melted and he laughed. "I'm actually trying to stop smiling like a crazed loon," he whispered back. "I'm—" *Happy.* He didn't know how to say the words.

"I'm happy too!" she confided.

What a woman. She read minds too. He ushered his princess in, selected a cotton-draped table, and pulled out her chair.

The serving girl twirled her pencil. "Got some fresh 'prairie oysters' today, sir."

Heath gagged a little. "Er…not fond of roasted calves' testicles."

"Chitterlings, then?" The girl began to scribble. He hastily shook his head.

Opal grinned at his no-doubt pale cheeks. "Only pigs' intestines. Where's that tough prospector now?"

He growled, "I'll get used to your strange American food one day."

They ate chicken-fried steak, potatoes, beans, and greens, and drank whiskey and water with their meal.

A crowd of western-clad folk came in on a gust of cool outside air. Three cowboys jingled in after them. Heath registered them all with the wary part of his mind, most of his attention focused on the charming and lovely Miss Opal Calahan as she chattered excitedly about her new play.

He was concentrating so hard on not wincing every time she said "play" or "drama," "costume," "orchestra," and "stage," that the whispers had turned to low-voiced bullets by the time they registered.

105

"*Claim jumper.*" From the cowboys' table. Snickers. Muttered oaths and ribald, half-drunken laughter.

"*Killed his partner.*"

"*Outlaw.*"

Heath manfully ignored them. He gave himself a greater pain to distract himself. "Very well. I'll gladly help you rehearse the hero's lines," he promised Opal, loving the light that brightened in her eyes. He couldn't refuse her anything. "Only rehearsing! No actually going to the...p-play."

Opal spat on her hand and held it out. "Deal!"

Background mutters and exclamations traversed the room like a brush fire. Circling closer. Heath's skin hunched and shivered under his Sunday best.

Suddenly a shrill woman's voice rang out, high-pitched and terrified. "*Murderer!*" she screamed. The woman stood, pointing a finger. "*Here in this very room!*"

The black wave crashed over him. Pain striated through his temples, his brain. He couldn't breathe, the vise on his chest tightened and tightened, wild screaming resounded on and on in his ears—he clung clawed hands to head, where was the exit, he had to get away—

Ballarat. Rocks hitting his back, his shoulders. Weeks of it now. His head jerked as a sharp stone bounced off his skull. He staggered, regained his feet, kept running with a shambling, stumbling run. Who had brewed this angry mob? Everyone hated him. *Claim jumper, bushranger, murderer, murderer—voices shrieking vitriol inside his head and out—*

A gunshot split the air. Heath snapped into the

present. The smell of cordite hung like smoke in the abrupt, shocked silence. The room darkened several shades.

Miss Opal Calahan stood, pistols in each hand. She'd shot the wicks from two candles in the candelabra above them all.

"Everybody," she said, "can just shut their gossiping traps."

The three cowboys jumped out of their seats. Two had pulled guns, but they were nowhere quick as Opal Calahan. Half the folk at the other table had crawled under the long tablecloth. Heath could see two large gingham-clad bottoms and one canvas backside protruding from the white cloth, shaking with fear.

A laugh bubbled up from nowhere. The black memories lost their grip and slid a little. He pushed them away with every bit of grit and determination he possessed, focusing hard on Opal.

The door burst open, and two hotel barmen stared wildly around, taking in the scene. The doorman rushed in after them, his eyes boggling at Opal.

When Heath could speak, he said, "Finished your dinner, my love? May I suggest this is an opportune time to find a venue which offers dancing."

Opal blew the bore of each of her pistols and replaced them in her skirts. She smiled sunnily. "I'd be delighted, Mr. Rawdon."

Together they stalked from the silent room, the doorman giving way, eyebrows raised.

Once around the corner in Sidewinder Lane, Heath and Opal flattened themselves against the wall of Jake's Place and cried with laughter.

Heath pulled the still-shaking Opal close to him.

"C'mon, gunslinger. We better go dancing before that story is all over town and we're barred from every respectable establishment."

"Ha! Nonsense. I'm sure there's a gunfight in Wylder Street every day, all those gun-totin' cowboys swinging around the place. This town just loves a drama. And I'm gonna make their wishes come true with the brand new, lit-up, grand Wylder Playhouse!"

He grinned at her. "Listen. The band is starting up just down the alley there at Five Star Saloon. Listen to those fiddles and that squeezebox! Does it make your toes tap, Opal?"

Her smile shone even in the darkness of the side street. "I'd be proud to take a waltz or a lively galop with you, Heath Rawdon. You sure scrub up mighty fine in your Sunday clothes, and I want to enjoy the night with such a handsome fellow. Let's go, pardner."

Lucky they'd be dancing, not talking. Heath wasn't sure he could get words out over the huge lump of emotion clogging his throat.

And lucky the darkness hid the hopeful, astonished tears prickling behind his eyes.

Opal had shot away his demons, with her quick, brave draw and her quick, brave heart.

Chapter Nine

The Five Star Saloon was a typical western joint, a little on the raw side but making up for that in a colorful, laughing crowd, jumping atmosphere, fast dance music, and plentiful grog. Doorways revealed card rooms for the gamblers and money launderers, the ranch hands come in from the wilds to burn up their wages and livers for the night, the wide-eyed greenhorns eager for their first taste of Wylder. Women of all kinds glowed like rainbow parrots amongst the cowboys, miners, gamblers, and wild men.

Kind of like what was best and worst about the Ballarat goldfields too.

Heath clasped Opal in a fast, whirling waltz; he was sure the Viennese would stare through their quizzing glasses should they spy this riotous gypsy version!

He held Opal's slender frame close to his own, enjoying her elastic athleticism as he guided her faster and faster, until she laughed, her chest heaving delightfully as she gasped for breath.

"I hope you don't get kicked out of the Vincent," Heath said as he propelled her to a tiny, vacant table for a drink and a rest. He didn't want to stop dancing, didn't want to release his clutch on her, but he judged she would enjoy a brief rest and refreshment.

He signaled to the waitress as he pulled the chair

for her.

"I only shot two candles out," Opal said, scornfully.

"Bullet hole in the white wall behind?"

"Ha! I bet that old hotel is half lead from gunplay, painted over white."

He snorted a laugh.

Opal regarded him as she gratefully took a few large gulps of her lemonade. "One more dance, and then I want to show you something."

Heath's body stirred. She doesn't want to show you soft white *skin*, he told his loins firmly. "Four more dances," he said aloud. "Sunday best, remember? Can't waste it."

She smiled teasingly, pretending to decide. "Three. And then you'll come and see. *And* you'll rehearse some lines at your camp tomorrow."

Heath held his hands up in mock surrender. "I suppose I must be grateful you actually paused to negotiate with me."

The smile on her face fled.

Alarm built in him as the glitter of tears sparkled in her eyes. "Opal, what did I say? Please. Was just a pathetic joke. I love your smile."

She drank more lemonade. Visibly battled with herself. Slammed her drink on the table. "Don't laugh. Don't soothe. Don't say no useless, meaningless words."

"I promise."

"*Hasty*. That's what my family says about me. Excitable, too fast on the draw, quick-tempered, thoughtless, heedless. Hasty. A very bad thing for a gunslinger to be."

He reached over and gripped her hand. A tear spangled her eyelashes, then slid down her pink cheek.

Words fought in his brain. Careful now. "Do you *want* to be a gunslinger?" He waited, heart thudding. Relief pooled through him as her expression cleared.

"No, not anymore. *I'm a playwright.* You are good for me, Mr. Heath Rawdon." She stood. "C'mon then, three quick spins."

And she was back in his arms, and all was right with the world.

****

Heath's skin shivered and jumped as they strolled along the star-lit Old Cheyenne Road, but no screaming women or angry mobs pursued him. Only imaginary stones hit between his shoulder blades. He pulled Opal closer, for her protection or his, he didn't care to analyze. She felt so good, swinging along next to him. He hunched into his shoulders and pulled his hat lower as they turned into a tiny back street toward Wylder Street. Forced himself to relax.

They meandered along the twisting lane, weaving between a blacksmith reeking of burned metal, a wagon shop redolent with wood shavings and paint, and a tiny timber church.

Heath peered into the shadows ahead. "Do you know where this alley leads?"

"I'm hoping I do. Didn't want to take you past the Vincent again, so we're going this exciting new back way."

What a woman. An iceberg thawed deep in his chest, and he lost breath for a moment. Such care of him. Not sure he'd ever known such softness, except maybe long ago as a boy. In his dreams.

The alley widened, and Heath and Opal stepped out into Wylder Street, right on the east edge of town.

There facing them stood a huge old mansion, from pioneer days maybe. Long abandoned, by the look of it. Hunching down into its haunches, weary of holding up its lace balconies and high ceilings, fancy plasterwork and grand portico all the long years. Under a high arch to the right of the mansion, a big carriage drive curled beyond, overgrown with weeds.

Then he saw Opal's face.

Alive with hope. Glowing like a beacon of dreams and desire. "Heath?" she whispered. "Marvelous, isn't it?"

Heath looked again. Rotting timbers. Peeling paint. Boarded-up window cavities. Reeking of mildew, mold, mayhem, and mud. But a warrior's heart lurked within that frame. A grand dame on her uppers.

A strange emotion uncurled within him, and his heartbeat picked up in a tattoo. Was that how she saw him? Through to the marrow? To the proud, determined man he once was?

And maybe could be again.

Heath swallowed. Whatever Opal Calahan wanted with this building, he would help her do it. "Your playhouse?" he asked, voice low. Hazarding a guess.

"Clever!" Opal flung her arms around him, then released him quickly, blushing confusion. "Errr. Hasty," she muttered. Brightened. "Yes, my brand-spanking-new Wylder Playhouse."

She faced him fully, gripped his hands and squeezed tight. "I'm going to restore this beauty. I'll write such plays for Wylder!" She shook him, unaware of what she did, Heath considered. He didn't mind.

Squeeze away, Opal.

"I'll show them! I'll show them! I'll prove them all wrong—I'm not hasty, it's my quicksilver creative temperament. My plays will be a famous, resounding success—you'll see! They'll *all* see."

She released him and fisted her right hand in the air. "I will do this! *I'll show them!*"

Both arms stretched up in a victory salute. She tossed her fine head back like a thoroughbred filly about to race in the Melbourne Cup.

"Bravo!" Heath regarded her glowing eyes and the high color in her cheeks. "And I'll help you. Learnt a bit over the years, shoring up mines, building plank huts. Like to work hard—it keeps the mad voices quiet."

Did he say that last bit out loud? Shocked, he looked closely at Opal for her reaction. Hunched his shoulders.

Her smile glinted in the starlight and the pools of mellow yellow candlelight and lamplight spilling from the Vincent Hotel down the road and the Wylder Hotel farther west. "Heath. I'm a writer, remember? My head is filled with yammering voices that get so urgent, I feel if I don't them write them quick, get them out fast on to the page, my brain will burst. I live every day with multiple voices rattling around in my head. You couldn't have said that to a perfecter person."

"Opal." He couldn't help himself. Such a wave of yearning and happiness combined surged through him. He bent his head toward hers. Grazed her plump lips with his own. Wanting her.

She moved slightly. Up toward him: invitation enough. Heath lowered his mouth, holding back his

113

greed, landing his lips gently, softly, on hers. He waited, barely touching. Breathing her in. He placed his hands carefully on her upper arms.

"Heath!" Her voice against his mouth, impatient. Bossy.

His own mouth curled in a smile. He pressed on her sweet lips. Tasting her. Giving and taking pleasure in that soft, sweet joining. He pulled her a little closer, her breasts grazing his chest. "Opal," he groaned and then licked the seam of her lips with the tip of his tongue until she parted for him. There, in front of the disheveled but soon to be loved and restored Wylder Playhouse, damaged Heath Rawdon, reclaimed, kissed his Opal passionately, thoroughly, completely.

He shook with need and passion. She was so vibrant, so whole and healing, so lovely.

A sudden noise startled him. Still holding Opal, he drew back. Stared at her, dazzled and wanting. Guilt and dismay flooded him in a poisonous rush. He opened his mouth.

"Don't you dare apologize, Heath Rawdon! We're in this together."

How he loved the sound of that.

She splayed a hand flat on his chest, probing the beating of his heart with curious fingers. "It's like a promise, see? My first kiss in front of my playhouse, with the fine, wonderful man who will help me get there."

"It is a promise. More than that. *A vow*." Heath's voice rasped over the jagged rocks in his throat. He might have failed his mate, back in Ballarat. He wouldn't fail Opal. He'd vowed it, on their first kiss.

The noise again. A sudden scraping, coming from

the rear.

Heath said, "Opal, I'll take you back to the Vincent Hotel." He resolutely squashed the fearful tremor that came with uttering the name of that hotel. He was on the other side of the world here. He was harder now, more desperate. Quicker to fight back. "I'll check out this old building a little more. Might be squatters living here, gamblers and hard men down on their luck."

"Well, I'm coming."

"Opal, no—" He laughed as she patted her skirts. "Sorry. I forget you've saved me twice now. What a woman you are." He said the last phrase softly. He had a lot of thinking to do. He didn't deserve her. He could hardly promise her a whole man.

But he could fix up her playhouse for her.

Why she wanted this old ruin...but he could see it. The building oozed charm, as well as mold and mildew. Had character deep in her elegant bones.

He gestured Opal to stick behind him, and they began to sneak along the dark side of the grand old building. Clang! Heath stepped on a pile of old bottles, and the glass rolled and crashed together, shattering the quiet of the night. Heath stopped, gripping Opal behind him, his heart thudding in his ribs.

Shots could come from anywhere. Opal would have no chance to draw.

"Let's go in from the front," Heath murmured. "We'll have light oozing in from the street to help us. Or come back tomorrow, in daylight."

"Sure. The front entrance. Let's do it now. Can't wait till tomorrow."

Heath bit back the "hasty" which found itself on his tongue. One small h escaped. Opal's face jerked around and glimmered at him for a moment.

She let it go.

Lucky for him she was excited about her playhouse.

He led the way to the front of the mansion and stepped warily up the formal but splintered and decaying front steps. The entrance opened into a high-ceilinged, grand space. He instantly saw Opal's vision. This place would make a brilliant playhouse—after about twenty years of hard work.

"Look at these beautiful tall ceilings," she whispered into the dimness. Heath wedged the door open, and light followed them in. "That grand stage there. Wooden rails over the top for stage curtains. Plenty of space leading back for backstage and actors' refreshment rooms. I'm sure this place used to be some theater or music hall, don't you think?"

"Looks like it. Wonder why it's abandoned?" A hundred reasons smashed through his brain, each one worse than the last.

"Waiting for its very own playwright to come to town!" she said, her excited tones bouncing around the echoing space.

"Keep it down," Heath said. A faint creaking alerted him. With well-honed reflexes, before his brain registered what he was doing, he grasped Opal and threw her across the space, hit the floor himself, rolling to a stop amid a pile of smelly rags in a corner.

Where they had been standing, a beam overhead gave a loud sigh and then smashed to the wooden floor with the impact of a runaway carriage hitting a brick wall. Running boots clattered loudly in the dimness, heading back into the depths of the ruined mansion.

Heath leaped to his feet, crouching and looking about him. "Opal!" Gave his Sunday best a cursory brush down and tore to where she sat in a stunned, crumpled heap, near a stack of mildewing chairs.

She heaved herself upright. "Someone just tried to loose a roof beam onto us. Tried to kill us. Did you see him?"

"I saw a black shape in the roof when I heard the sound. Come on, back to the hotel. You've had a fright." He put his arm around her. "It was a warning."

"Rubbish," Opal retorted fiercely, pulling out of his embrace. "I'm made of sterner stuff, Heath Rawdon, and the sooner you know it, the better. This is my Wylder Playhouse. Let's root out this viper and kill him." She brushed at the bodice of her dress, magnetizing Heath's gaze, switched her skirts into place, and stalked off into the dark hallway.

A thousand agitated ideas pummeled his frantic skull as he stared after her. Grab her and bodily carry her back to the Vincent? Why would someone push a roof beam on them? A desperate squatter? Or had they been followed—did they know who Heath was and want him out of the way so they could grab his claim? *Gold fever*. Drove men to desperate acts of savagery.

"Opal," he hissed. The wench wasn't coming back to safety. Did she think she was unstoppable? Blast all gunslingers. Reckless. Crazy. Foolhardy. *Hasty*. He gritted his teeth and marched into the dark maw of a hallway.

The stench of rot and mildew wafted in his nose. Ouch! Obstacles to smash unwary shins rose in the darkness. He limped forward, trailing his fingers along the wainscoted walls for direction and balance. Peeling

117

wallpaper above.

A sudden noise. A door slamming. A woman's shriek cut off. "Heath—" Loud bump.

Heath ran.

He skidded into a large back room, light filtering weakly through broken blinds. A tall dark form held a wriggling, kicking Opal tight against him. Metal gleamed against her pale throat. She stilled.

"Let her go." Heath's voice was heavy with warning. He flashed a quick scan around the room, looking for weapons, exits, options. The shape didn't speak. He was shrouded in shadow, a hat pulled low over his face. Black clothes. Scent of...metal. Desert soil.

Heath's heart pinged with warning. Outlaw. Hunted man. They'd disturbed him in his hideout.

"Get your hands off her," Heath snarled. Stepped closer. The knife arm shifted in. Hell, was that a thin line of Opal's blood? Couldn't see in the hazy darkness. He halted, fury burning in him like an inferno.

The man still didn't speak. Nothing.

That gave Heath a clue. *Maybe they knew him.* His voice would give him away. A man with an accent? Distinctive voice? Speech impediment of some kind?

"What do you want, monster?" Opal shrieked suddenly, kicking him hard in the shins. The knife jumped. And so did Heath. He shoved Opal out of the way again and tackled the tall man, felling him to the ground.

They rolled over and over on the floor, a mess of fighting, wrestling limbs, battling for supremacy. "Don't shoot!" he shouted to Opal.

The man gained ascendancy over Heath, staring

down at him with eyes that glittered evilly in the darkness. He raised a fist as though to hammer Heath's nose; Heath bucked and threw the lean figure. The man tore himself from under Heath's furious fist, in three strides reached the open window, and vaulted through, vanishing into the night.

Opal ran to Heath. He opened his arms, and she collided into him, shaking and gibbering. In a remarkably short time, she calmed. Heath held her tight. They both glanced around the room.

"Set up for a camp," Opal said, wonder in her voice as she gestured to a neat bed in one corner, table and rickety chair, small spirit stove, wooden box with spare clothes and a worn book. "We better tell the sheriff, but he's not gonna be happy with me."

A smile somehow found Heath. "For which bit? Associating with a wanted, murdering claim jumper? Burgling an old mansion on the edge of town? Shooting up a respectable hotel and frightening the dinner patrons?"

Opal laughed. "Thunderation! When you put it like that, it does sound kinda rowdydow. Maybe we better not tell the sheriff."

"What we need to do," Heath said, injecting grit, "is discover who actually owns this old place. We can't eject any squatters until you own it, Opal Calahan."

"Oh." Her musical voice went quiet and flat. "Good point." In the dim light, he watched her deflate, watched all that sass and zest leach out of her like yesterday's balloons.

"It's gonna cost a bomb, isn't it?" She stared down at her toes, despair and grief emanating from her in waves. She slumped, held her body very still in a posture of defeat. Before Heath could move in, ask what troubled her, offer comfort, she shook her head. Kicked a table leg viciously and stood tall and straight.

"Easily fixed," she said, conviction ringing in her voice. "I know what I have to do."

"Opal?"

She whispered, "I have to take a job."

For a second, Heath hardly knew what she meant. Then it dawned. "Opal, no!"

"Kill a man. Best him in a gunfight." She shaped her empty hand into a pistol grip and aimed it at the window.

A lightning crack of certainty smote Heath Rawdon. Not on his watch. Not his sweet, happy, lively Opal...even if she won, what would it do to her?

Heath put his arm around her. She let him this time. Allowed him to walk her out of that dark dangerous fantasy and back into the light.

"No, you won't," Heath promised. "I'll find gold. Soon. You will have your playhouse." He gripped her hard. Make her look at him. "Opal, please. Just wait a little. I'm so close..."

She gazed back. Spat on her hand, held it out, solemn as a priest. "Done. Three weeks."

Heath spat on his. "Done." Even if he had to work as if possessed by the devil himself.

As they neared the Vincent Hotel, he gave into an overmastering impulse. He pulled her into the laneway. Fought the urge to kiss her.

"Opal," he said. Even he heard the hoarseness. But she didn't flee. She *trusted* him. "Where'd you get the money for this venture?"

"I earned it."

"The second time we met. You said—you hinted—you'd been on a job, with your brother Burnley."

"You listened! And remembered." Her eyes glowed in the starlit dimness.

He squinted around in the dark alley, watched a skinny black cat slinking in from Wylder Street, imagined dirt and trash blown up against the building walls. "I better take you somewhere comfortable, and—"

"Heath. I'm fine here, in the dark, with you." Her lovely smile shone out of the gloom.

"Here, sit on me." He slithered down the wooden wall, parking his bum on who knew what, but giving Opal a clean sturdy place to sit. His warmth if she needed it. "Can you tell me?"

She nestled closer. Her body cleaved to his as she took a huge breath. "I shot an evil man. I took a bad job so I could be free. Be me. I accepted a contract and harmed a man."

"Speak, Opal." He lightly stroked her neck under her hair.

"With my older brother Burnley. A straight contract. Ride into town, issue a challenge, main street, guns at dawn. I was brought up to that life. Thought I'd be *good*. Wanted to impress Burnley, too, I guess. From the moment I could toddle after him, I worshipped my older brother."

He repressed a sharp spike of jealousy. Her *brother*, you flaming pink galah.

Long silence.

Heath gave her the time she needed. His strength supported her. "You're safe," he said softly. "I'm of no account. An outlaw with a price on my head. Nobody

121

believes a word I utter."

He sensed her swallow and struggle with herself. She raised her chin, staring blindly up at the sliver of stars above. "We all stood in the middle of that old street. Started pacin' out the requisite twenty paces. Well, maybe you can guess what happens next."

"Opal. A thousand endings."

She glimmered a smile up at him, eyes misty. "Now you know what it's like inside my head all the time."

He laughed. Hell, that felt good. *She* felt good.

Opal's voice came tight as a bow string. "We paced. Then I sensed it. A quiver in the air. A sigh behind a shuttered window. Something. So I turned at only fifteen paces—and caught a glimpse of one o' them pistoleros turning too. Maybe he couldn't count past fifteen. His right arm. Then the silver shine as his gun pointed at Burnley."

She inhaled. "I had less than a split second—so I drew and shot that shark in his gun arm. He dropped the weapon and hollered. Burnley whipped round real fast—I thought he'd shoot me instead of the bandit, he was so mad. Burnley cleaned up the other varmint."

Opal wriggled around, causing all kinds of sensations in him. Her pretty lips shone so close to his. Her breath warmed his chest and neck. "I shot to protect my brother. We collected our winnings, but we only got half as witnesses said I fired too soon. Burnley ripped strips off me, callin' me hasty."

"Probably embarrassed you saved him."

"Burnley? Nah…" Pause. "And I *hated* it. Harming a man for money. Vowed never, ever to do it again. But to save Burnley? Even with him mad at me, I'd do it again. No hesitation."

She laughed, a sad, soft sound. "Then all my family—'cept Neddy—got into the habit of callin' me hasty, everything I tried."

"Let me get this straight. Your first time on a job, you disabled a renowned gunfighter, saved your eldest brother's life, and your whole family criticized you?"

"More teased. But yes."

"You're not hasty, Opal. Loyal, quick-witted, fast-acting. Your brother is lucky—and alive."

"When you put it that way…! Then reality came crashing in. With my earnings, I ran from the gunslinging life. I must make recompense for my grave deed by bringing people pleasure. With plays. *And* I must be successful so my youngest brother Neddy never has to take another gunslinger job. His gift for math and angles makes him a precise shot—but he lacks the will for the money shot. That'll kill him, faster 'n you can say 'sharpshooter.' "

She ran a hand over Heath's arm and his whole body lit with sparks. She mused, "A sliver of time, a choice, and the world changes. You're dead. Or injured for life. Or cursed with corroding regret."

"Yes." Grimness weighted the skin on his cheeks. "The world pivots on such moments." He held her. "Are you corroding inside with regret?"

She wriggled again. Her teeth shone white. "No! For Burnley, someone I love, to save them? I'll draw my pistol, always and every time! No question, no hesitation, and blast regret!"

He squeezed her to him, his valiant, huge-hearted, gorgeous gunslinger.

He cleared his choked throat. "Those pivotal

moments come. What counts is what we do with them. I tried, Opal, I tried. For years. But I never found my mate, and in the end, I couldn't bear the world's hatred, scorn, and vitriol."

They stood. Heath brushed down Opal's dress with his hands, taking his time over it. Then he watched from the shadows of Jamison's apothecary while she crossed the road to the lit-up Vincent Hotel.

Kept guard as she ascended the steps, stopping to apologize prettily to Parkinson, who touched his cap and bowed, clearly dazzled by Miss Opal Calahan.

He watched the last ruffle of her skirt vanish into the hotel.

Heath walked his way back to his lonely claim, down the side alleys, over the Medicine Bow Bridge and along the dusty track to his camp. He gazed up at the great arch of sky, heavy with bright stars, sparkling in constellations foreign to his southern hemisphere eyes. But still glorious, for all that.

Sometimes a man could believe in mighty fate, on a starry night like this.

He was a different man from the one who had arrived here. Now, his heart sang with a secret.

He loved Miss Opal Calahan, with all the capacity of his blackened, bruised, cracked, and withered heart. He could feel it expanding painfully, like a seed after sweet spring rain.

And if he'd never had that that horrible, dreadful, harmful experience in Ballarat, he never would have met her.

Chapter Ten

"Heath Rawdon!" That sweet voice could summon him from hell itself.

As perhaps she had done, he thought, as sunlight hit his mud-caked, wet shirt, vest, and trousers, and boots twice their normal size with sticky mud all over them.

Two long days since their night dancing and adventuring at the playhouse.

Days he'd worked his mine from before sunup to the last streaks of daylight in the sky, then hammered and sawed in that moldering playhouse by lantern light. He must find gold before she killed a man. Or got kil—

He coughed. Slammed the black box over those thoughts.

"You promised!" she chirped, fresh as a spring wildflower in a yellow checked dress. Matching yellow bows in her hair made him want to groan aloud. His old fella pulsed in his trousers, despite their clingy wetness.

"I promised a lot of things, Miss Opal," he said, stacking tools so he didn't feel so embarrassed.

"Rehearsals," she announced. "C'mon, you'll do, just like that. Unless you'd like to change? Here—I brought you fresh clothes, all washed and hot pressed by the Vincent maids."

Now he did groan aloud, almost in ecstasy. What she said next made him shut his eyes in a prayer of

125

gratitude.

"And here's some hot meals, fresh from the Vincent's kitchen, with meat and vegetables and barley. Apples. Bread." She bustled about, putting things away.

Normally he hated people at his camp, looking at his things. He'd get a prickly rush of possessive fury, feel wary and violated. But Opal?

Look at her bending over, tucking his hot meals in his cast iron camp oven to stay warm. Placing apples in a pretty straw basket laid invitingly on a stump.

Suddenly, the camp looked like a home.

His throat closed over. Something sharp melted in his chest. His cheeks crumpled into a forlorn, grateful, loonish yearning…his mouth hung open with need.

Luckily for his dignity, next she said crisply, "You'll be reading the hero's lines."

His skin jumped. Panic hit his limbs, like he'd been doused in a bucket of freezing water. She sauntered close, smiling at him in that special Opal way, intent, smiling, curious. Utterly delicious in her yellow checked dress. "I wrote some extra special hero lines for you, Heath Rawdon. I simply cannot *wait* to hear you say them."

He narrowed his eyes at her. "Don't get any ideas. I'll repair that place for you, much as I can. Treat it like any building project. But I will *not* go anywhere near that stage!"

Temper rose in her delicious round cheeks. Those jewel eyes sparked fire. "All you have to do is say a few lines!"

"No, Opal, I don't. I said I'd practice those lines for you, so you can hear how they sound. I'm not your leading man."

Suddenly, the sticky, damp mud seemed to squeeze all over him. He felt cold, and angry, and impatient. "I'm not your leading man in any way! This is just you being *hasty* and foolish. I'm dangerous, a wanted man, a rough nut, a *bastard of a bloke*." He strode to his tools, hoiked up a pick, threw it against a skinny desert tree.

"Look at me. Two nights ago, I got lured into one of your fantasies—" He gestured wildly around. "But this is me. *This is me*. I'll find your gold. But you need to find another leading man. In every way."

Nostrils flaring, blood pounding in his head, he stared at her.

Her sweet lips quivered. Her eyes were very shiny. She gazed back, hurt whitening her lovely round cheeks. She swallowed a lump in her throat. Looked totally desolated.

"It's not a game, Opal. Not a story," he ground out, gritty as the desert shale.

She threw a big heap of white pages down on the muddy ground.

She turned and walked away.

And he watched her go.

When she was completely out of sight, he ran around, rescuing the pages where they were being blown around by the sage-scented breeze and collected them in a tidy pile.

He put them carefully in a clean leather folder and stored them in his tent.

Later, he ate a hot meal, staring gloomily as single bright stars pricked the pastel-streaked sky, behind the lonely peaks of the Medicine Bow mountains.

****

Something had stolen Opal's stomach and replaced it with a sack of writhing, stinging snakes, and filled her legs with pins. She stumbled back to Wylder town, half blinded by tears and fury. Her brain pounded and screamed like a train in a tunnel.

What had she been imagining? That they'd rehearse the hero's lines, there in the beautiful, lonely desert, just she and the handsome, wounded prospector, and then...

Heath would kiss her.

She'd imagined it all, so vivid her breath caught in her throat: his strong body enclosing hers, his strength held to gentleness as he touched her. His muscular, lean body holding her softness close against him. His lips, flirting with hers, landing firm and wanting, on her mouth.

His tongue flicking at the corner of her lips, like he did the other day, tangling and sliding against hers.

She'd got it all so wrong.

"I'll show him!" she shouted at the Medicine Bow River rushing under the footbridge. "Curse all proud, stubborn fools of men." She stepped off the bridge and walked to the steep riverbank, slipping down on shale and pebbles to crouch at the water's edge. She scooped up handfuls of water where it looked cleanest, to bathe her stinging eyes and cool her hot cheeks.

"Bluebell and I will do it without him. Plenty of good leading men here in this town. A surfeit of cowboys who'll act in my play for a lark."

Her usual ebullient spirits partially restored, she tossed her hair, straightened her shoulders, and marched like a warrior maiden into the fray.

****

128

"You need to go *today*?" Opal stared at her assistant. "We've got to organize this play in a hurry, Bluebell, and I'm counting on you."

"Sorry, miss." The girl's patent misery tore at Opal's heart. "I won't go if you need me that much. I kinda hoped...three days wouldn't hurt—" The quavering voice subsumed into a loud sniffle.

"Bluebell, now you work for me, you blow your nose on a handkerchief, rather than your sleeve—that way it stays clean. Cleaner. Here." Opal waited for the loud blowing, snorting, and huffing to calm to a jerky sniff. "Why do you need to go home today?"

Heath's warning flashed through her mind: because the girl had thieved half Opal's possessions and now wanted to lam off?

Nonsense.

"The twins' birthday, miss. They's only five. Five!" Bluebell's expression lightened, and a smile broke through the misery like sun after rain. "I've kept..." She swallowed. Fresh tears sprouted. She whispered, "I've saved a whole half-eagle to give Ma so they can have a present each and a little party for everybody. Pay some rent too. Hold off eviction for another few weeks."

Her tear-stained cheeks pinked. "I saved it, though that mean witch gen'rally docked my pay for damages."

Guilt slithered in Opal's guts. She grabbed her assistant and pulled her tight in an impulsive embrace. Shed a few salty tears herself. "Bluebell, of course you must go! Now, do you have the fare?"

Bluebell shook her head. "I thought to cadge a lift from a farmer or cowboy. Walk as far as I could."

"Here. You can take the stage coach. Much safer.

Make sure you buy a pie from Cissy's bakery so you can eat on the way. I'll see you back here in five days."

"*Five* days? Miss. No! I haven't done any work for you yet—"

"Take it." She kissed the girl's forehead. "With my blessing."

Bluebell scrambled her meager goods together and, with a starry expression, bid Opal farewell and hastened away.

Opal counted the coins left in her purse. Dwindling fast. Maybe she still had enough to call her baby brother Neddy here to help her to restore the playhouse—once she discovered who owned it.

He was her youngest brother, and she had to save him.

If she got too low on funds, she'd take a job.

Her whole body shuddered. She hunched her shoulders, repulsed. She'd take a job to hunt a wanted killer. Shoot to incapacitate. The thought of killing anyone filled her with loathing.

Pity they didn't take women as lawmen. She'd join the sheriffs or federal marshals and earn money in a legitimate way. She could look after her growing list of dependents.

Marshal. She hadn't told Heath. The outlaw in the playhouse, as he'd pressed her against his stringy, stinking form, had almost knocked her out with a rank smell of unaired leather, rusty metal, and horse. That particular sour waft struck a strange chord in her memory—one that brought Adder Jackson, the snake-eyed federal, to mind.

But as hard as she grabbed after the wisp of memory, it vanished.

130

No matter. Things to do. *Urgent.*

She rushed off a quick letter to her feckless youngest brother, asking him to come and help her at Wylder. She didn't say, *before you get your foolish carcass killed.* She blew on the page to dry the ink and went downstairs to give to a hotel man to post.

No marriage to Buck Standish, no Heath, no leading man, no assistant, no playhouse—yet—her first play thrown in the mud, and very soon, no money.

Ya better get shootin', Opal Calahan, or you'll be heading home to work in the family business and have to marry some horrid ol' triggerman.

She knew what her da and brothers would say about her ill-informed, disastrous mission.

Far. Too. Hasty.

****

Opal spent two feverish hours blocking out a new play with a miner hero who looked and behaved remarkably like Heath Rawdon. She screwed up three pages and threw them at the wall, then gave in to her creative muse. The cowboys could fake a down-under accent.

Next, she ran around town marshaling her actors. She organized new pamphlets and posters in a whirlwind of hopeful zing.

Next Saturday—one night only!
The Gunslinger and the Rose
The Wylder Playhouse, Wylder Street
Tickets at the door. 7:00 p.m. start
Fifty cents to the floor and one dollar to the gallery
Enquiries: Miss Opal Calahan, Playwright
Vincent House Hotel.

She visited the newspaper office, the post office, stage coach office, the rail office, and the telegraph office, asking the same question: Who owns the grand old building on the east end of Wylder Street, right on the edge of town?

And got as many different answers as folk she spoke to.

"Building is probably abandoned," the steely-eyed postmistress Essie Baumgardner said.

She went back to the newspaper office. Paid for a fortnight of ads, asking the owner of the building to contact her urgently.

Well, she'd tried. So she'd just fix it up and use it for her play anyhow.

So much to do. She needed Bluebell. A smile flitted over her face as she imagined the girl's return with money and presents for her numerous family and a few dresses of Opal's for her sisters to make over. A warm sensation in her heart summoned a smile.

Back to work.

****

Heath smashed out furious long hours of hard physical work each day, powered with the twanging buzz of angry frustration. Find gold. Find gold. Find gold.

The words sang in his blood, matching every beat of his heart.

Once darkness crawled over the land, sending its inky fingers around his camp and into his new mines, he packed up, cleaned up, ate a cursory meal, enough to keep his strength, grabbed his tool box, and rode Blue into Wylder, through the back lanes to the east edge of town.

Daylight was for finding gold.

Nighttime was for fixing up Opal's dream. Her Wylder Playhouse.

Heath was on a mission. He'd seen Opal's posters around town. He'd fix up that playhouse—at least the main theater—so it could function by Saturday. Four days.

Each evening, he saw where Opal had cleaned out the old mansion. Tonight, the front steps gleamed, the hallway had been swept and polished, and years of spiderwebs, litter, dust, and dead insects cleaned away. Looked like he'd been wrong about Bluebell—she must be a good worker.

Dusty footprints of all shapes and sizes crisscrossed the wide, ornate foyer. So the cast had begun rehearsing there. He must get the theater ready.

In the grand theater room, seats had been brushed down and walls cleaned, but the stage was still filthy and the thick old curtain hung bedraggled and dropping from its half-rotten beam. Heath eyed the beam that had nearly taken out him and Opal. Too heavy for the two women to drag away. He'd clear that first thing, then start on the stage.

He'd put in new floorboards to patch the holes in the wooden stage floor. Hammer in new boards to cover broken walls. Cut and sand a sturdy new curtain rod. Clean out the roof, so unpleasant items didn't fall on the actors' unwary heads, mid-play.

First though, he crept cautiously through the dark hallways to the rear of the mansion. He didn't like the thought of Opal working here, even in the day, even with Bluebell.

Guns or no, anything could happen to her.

He had to clean the vermin from its nest.

He pulled all the outlaw's gear out and left it in the yard. He considered setting fire to it, but that went against his grain. He'd leave it for the sinister stranger to remove. The man still needed his bed and stove. If he left Opal alone, Heath had no argument with him.

Heath returned to the main theater, set up his lanterns so he could operate in the darkness, and began work. Sawing, hammering, drilling, and sanding. The work hurt muscles already tired with mining, but it felt good too. The scent of fresh-hewn wood began to subsume rot and neglect.

Opal would have her playhouse.

He repressed the urgent, panicky pang about his claim.

Here he was in a playhouse. Leaving his claim unguarded.

History *would not* repeat.

****

Opal arrived the next morning, hauling two heavy buckets of hot soapy water and hung about with brooms, brushes, sponges, and old flour sacks to carry out trash, banging into her hips and legs.

She hustled up the front steps and into the theater—and stopped, mouth open.

The large beam lying diagonally across the floor, pinning rubbish beneath it, had been removed. She squinted her eyes into the dimness, dropped her loads on the floor, and edged forward.

The old, creaking stage, full of holes, had all been patched up with new boards. The back walls, formerly riddled with gaps that she'd thought to cover with cloth, had all been repaired. A long, wooden curtain rod stretched from one end of the roof beams to the other, ready for a new curtain.

And on the floor, just there right in front of the stage, a giant shape had been drawn in the thick gray dust.

A big love heart.

****

Heath was exhausted from his day and night work. That was why he didn't hear the evil marshal when he got to the camp.

Metal clanged. Loud thumps resounded and shook the walls of the mine he was hacking with his pick. Heath scurried up the ladder, his shoulder muscles shrieking with pain.

He burst out of the mine.

Adder Jackson was laying waste to his camp, throwing dishes, smashing Heath's stove, ripping at his tent until it collapsed in a lopsided heap.

Opal's play manuscript was in there!

He didn't waste another second, but sprinted to Adder Jackson and leapt on him with a roar of rage. The marshal might try to arrest him for violence. He'd have to catch him first.

The marshal and Heath fought, rolling over and over on the filthy ground, aiming hard blows at each other's faces. The lawman was hard and experienced, but Heath had the wild goldfields behind him.

He landed a mighty punch on the Adder's beaky nose. Blood spurted in a bright fountain. "I'm surprised your blood is red," Heath growled.

The trap clapped a hand to his bloody nose, writhing away from Heath, and pulled himself upright. "Stay out of my business, prospector," Adder Jackson hissed. "This is your last warning. I want you gone from here." He pulled a ragged scrap of newsprint from his pocket, tan with age. "If you are still here Saturday, that's it, felon. I'm arresting you."

"On what charge?"

"Disturbing the peace."

Heath held his arms wide. "Nobody could be more peaceful than me, *Marshal*. I'm bothering nobody." He stepped closer. Enjoyed a small pulse of satisfied rage as the Adder shrank back. "I'm staying until I've done my five years and got my land grant. Hear me, Marshal? You've got nothing to arrest me for."

The Adder swiped at his bloody nose. "Saturday," he repeated thickly.

Heath watched the lawman mount his tall black steed and ride away on the track toward the high mountain pass, the canyon, and the caves.

Strange the marshal hadn't brought cronies, if he wanted to give Heath a scare. Normally the law came in bully gangs, if they wanted to rough up a man and his camp, enough to make him flee.

So the Adder wanted to keep it low key. He hoped to run Heath out of town with nobody else knowing about it.

The marshal wanted him gone because he was up to something.

The law of the bush said keep your head down; mind your own business; render assistance when needed, but otherwise see nothing, say nothing, don't interfere. Heath raised his pick high and slammed it into the earth.

Then he turned his head and squinted into the distance.

Maybe the Adder wanted Heath's claim.

But it looked more like something to do with that canyon pass.

Chapter Eleven

Saturday evening! The night Opal Calahan claimed her future as Wylder's playwright.

Bluebell had arrived that morning, glowing and full of chatter, from the early stagecoach. She had diligently—more or less—learned her lines as leading lady while on her holiday. As Opal and her assistant made a final tour and check of the new Wylder Playhouse that morning, the girl had spouted such fulsome praise of the rushed transformation, that Opal's heart sang within her. Tonight!

The search for the owner yielded nothing. Some original old pre-Wylder family, people said. Died out, maybe.

The postmistress Essie Baumgardner had yesterday scribbled out a note to ask an aging spinster, the last of her line, who lived out in the backwoods in splendid isolation; Delphina Matilde Treadway might know. Opal paused in the restored auditorium as the memory flashed—an outrageous elderly woman dashing through Wylder in a gilded blue coach.

And now the ticket-paying crowd milled outside, chatter and laughter floating on the air like streamers. Excitement hummed. Cowboys, opera girls, hard mining men from the hills, hotel staff who'd begged a rare night off, business owners strutting in their best Sunday garb, travelers, even the sheriff, cheeks puffed

138

out and a lawman frown not quite disguising his happy anticipation, they'd all come.

She'd made enough money to stretch her stay at the Vincent, adding another two weeks.

Inside, a western band tuned up and cracked jokes in the orchestra pit below the stage. Wild street children turned stage hands chased each other through the theater. Laughter oozed from stage wings from the unseen actors. As Opal stood in the darkened theater, heart flying to the rafters and stomach churning and knotting with terror and elation, the main door opened, spilling light.

Her first audience members came tripping up the aisle: almost the entire Vincent Hotel staff. She rushed to Molly Maguire and kissed both cheeks. "Thank you for coming! Thank you!"

"Whist now, brush away those tears, and give us a performance to remember."

Time for the show!

Opal fled to the rear stage, flitting from actor to actor. She wiped nervous tears from the girl from the Wylder County Social Club, Garnet, and gave her a quick hug. She slapped the backs of two cowboys, Leroy and Quentin, and smiled at a third, Driver. She grabbed one of the mischievous triplets, Sparrow Sagebrush, before he tumbled from a ledge he'd somehow climbed.

"Thank you, everybody. Tonight, Wylder comes into its own. Act your hearts out! Tonight, we fandango!"

Amidst the rousing cheers, Opal crept to the front of the stage and peered through the gap in the curtains. The spotlights lit the audience. Her gaze racked the crowd…

No goldminer, not muddy and disheveled coming at the last moment, or spruced up and tidy, having taken the afternoon to prepare himself. She slipped out of the wings and walked down the aisle at the edges of the audience seating. The room was warm, filled with perfume and hair oil, bodies and movement.

No prospector. No Heath. A slash of angry pain lanced her chest. Grief and fury bubbled in a nauseous mix in her belly.

What was she doing, mooning after someone who clearly didn't care, who should be here on her night of triumph?

She had work to do. She put up her chin, walked back to the stage, and gave the signals.

The western band struck up. The audience lights dimmed amid cheering and catcalls, then anticipatory silence.

The curtains opened on her first scenes, a cowboy swaggering into town.

The audience applauded and wolf-whistled. Opal's heart swelled within her. Her triumphant grin stretched from ear to ear. Fizz sizzled in her veins.

The first scenes were brilliant. Funny, heartwarming, colorful…the butterflies in her belly danced with glee. She could feel her glorious future unrolling before her dazzled eyes. When Quentin danced with Bluebell, she thought her heart would burst in victory.

Then—

Disaster struck.

A black bear cub tumbled onto the stage just as the cast assembled for the crowd scene. *What? A bear cub!*

Opal ran onto the stage, hoping she'd look part of the crowd scene, her eyes popping from her head, making hopelessly ineffective herding motions toward the gamboling cub. Holy moly, was its *mother* somewhere nearby?

Garnet spotted the bear cub and screamed blue murder. Two cowboys pulled guns, and large, loud Olive Sagebrush barreled onto the stage from the wings, shouting at the top of her considerable voice, "Put those guns away, now! Winter Sagebrush, come here!"

Laughter rang from the audience—so far, they all believed this to be scripted.

Two of the triplets toddled on stage, following their mother, who slammed a gun from Driver the cowboy's hand before he could shoot the cub, simultaneously hollering, "Moon Sagebrush! Get down from there!"

Opal's horrified gaze snapped onto a triplet scaling *the stage curtain*! Followed by one of his brothers, who fell and began sobbing noisily in distress. She stared helplessly around. A harassed Nartan Sagebrush, the Arapaho leather tanner, boomed in a fatherly stentorian voice across the hubbub, but his wild family ignored him. He scooped up the sobbing triplet.

Half her cast were herding the bear cub, while Olive Sagebrush dealt disciplinary blows indiscriminately. The western band, initially shocked into silence, ripped into a spritely hoedown dance tune, completely departing from the musical score.

The audience by now were standing in their seats, booing, hissing, yelling abuse, or catcalling and shrieking with laughter, depending on their temperament. A stampede for the exit door commenced

141

from one aisle. A bottle pinged from the audience and hit Quentin, who blasphemed loudly and leapt nimbly from the stage to wreak retribution on his attacker. More missiles from the enraged audience pelted cast members or landed on the stage, making it slippery and hazardous. The bear cub still ran amok. Half her cast had fled, the others were climbing the stage scenery or milling about, not knowing what to do.

A bottle hurtled through the air and hit Leroy on his cowboy hat. He pulled his gun and shot into the roof, accompanied by wild shrieking and cursing by the outraged audience.

The sheriff appeared, climbing on stage from the audience, and raised his voice and his hands until he had gained control of the situation.

And to seal to the disaster that was her first play, Leroy's shot, or perhaps the climbing triplets, unmoored the stage curtain. With a sound like the crack of doom, the heavy red curtain split from its beam and fell, covering most of the remaining cast, the bear cub, and the sheriff.

Her first play was an unmitigated, horrific disaster.

Opal stood on the stage, summoning every scrap of courage. "You'll all get your money back!" she shouted into the riot on stage and in the auditorium. "Apply at the Vin—" Slap! A great clod of mud hit her on the cheek. So she just stood there, feeling like the greatest fool, as chaos reigned all around her.

"You need to prepare a little better, Miss Calahan," a high-pitched voice snapped in her ear. "You can put on your next play in about fifty years, when you've learned how to plan in a proper manner." Opal looked wearily around. Mrs. Andrews, stiff curls still rigid even in this madness, her lips stretched downward in haughty disdain. Oh, Lord save her. Bluebell's tormentor. Helmet woman.

Opal watched the old horror march away. At the exit, the dreadful woman turned back, her voice floating piercingly loud over the hubbub: "Far. Too. Hasty."

"I'd have to agree, Miss Calahan."

Opal looked miserably at the lawman. "I'm sorry, Sheriff. I didn't mean any of this to happen."

He nodded and patted her arm kindly, then returned to imposing a semblance of order.

Her playwright dreams lay in tatters all over the destroyed stage floor.

****

"Never, in the history of play disasters, has there been such a disaster as Opal Calahan's first, hasty play." She paced around the prospector's camp. She'd run all the way there in the night, to find him unaccountably gone.

Where else could she go? She was far too embarrassed to return to the Vincent, in case a crowd waited to hurl missiles at her. Excruciating. The whole of Wylder had seen her spectacular failure. So she'd run to the place outside of society, to the man who seemed to understand her, despite their many differences.

With whom she unaccountably felt anchored. Safe. Home.

But the blasted man wasn't here.

She paced around, heaving tools and throwing rocks randomly into the darkness, burning off grief, embarrassment, and fury in a whirlwind of nervous energy.

"And why weren't you watching my play?" she

shouted to the night. "Didn't you care? Did you think I'd fail?—as I did, most spectacularly. Why weren't you there on the most important night of my life?"

She hunkered down as the explosion of grief finally caught up to her. Heath didn't care. Nobody did. She'd made a great fool of herself, living ridiculous dreams, with no basis in reality.

Worse, she'd made promises. To Bluebell. She'd already written to her little brother, and he might even now be on his way. She'd have to refund all those tickets. Maybe even pay some kind of damages.

She punched her own forehead over and over, welcoming the pain of her own sharp knuckles. "Rash, stupid, foolish, romantic, idiot woman!"

After a long while, Opal decided to make a hot drink. Maybe stay out here, alone in the wilderness. The great dome of starry sky did offer a kind of absolution, a peace, as though her great worldly problems were mere pinpricks in the great river of time.

Sitting there alone, her hands cupped around a warm half mug of tea, she gazed spellbound up at the warrior constellation, Orion. Somehow that great hunter gave her comfort. Warriors made mistakes. Warriors tried. And failed. And tried again.

She idly picked up the folded paper that had rested under the mug on the stump. She smoothed it out and squinted at the writing there.

What? Addressed to her.

Opal, the note read. *If I don't come back for a few days, send the sheriff to search for me in the canyon caves. I'm following that so-called marshal. He gave me an ultimatum: be gone by Saturday.*

So Heath had deserted her! Anger smacked her that

he'd leave rather than support her, rather than see her play—childish anger.

The words on the note penetrated her heaving emotions. She re-read it. *Canyon caves. Following that so-called marshal. So-called.* Something buzzed in her brain again. She had met a man very like the so-called marshal...knowledge from long ago, a fear-ridden child staring up at a tall, tall man, a dark night and bright flashes of gun fire...but maybe she was mixing it all up.

Canyon caves...

Perfect. That's exactly what she needed. Action. She'd sneak back to town, hire a horse from the livery, and go search that canyon pass.

Heath must have been worried if he left a note for her. Her heart, so chilled with failure, warmed again. He needed her. She'd help him.

No use asking the sheriff. After tonight's debacle, the lawman wouldn't believe a word she said. And who could blame him?

He'd be still busy calming the storm she'd created.

There. Without even being here, Heath Rawdon had cheered her once again. Opal rushed back to town via the back lanes, filled with new purpose.

****

These canyon paths were sure spooky in the night, even with the moon almost full to light the way like a beacon. Visions of Heath's battered body possessed her mind now. Why had he gone? *Why hadn't he returned?* What had happened to him?

The only sounds were the steady clip-clop of her hired mountain pony, Sweetie, which she'd rechristened from Surly. Nobody deserved to be branded forever with a name like that. She patted Sweetie's neck, more

145

to reassure herself than the horse. Patted her pistols, holstered high on her hips for a quick draw.

A distant coyote's bone-chilling howl split the still air. The sound of heavy, flapping, invisible wings echoed in the canyon. Opal shivered. Bats?

She stopped at the canyon cave Heath had shown her. Relief and fresh panic intermingled—Blue! She tied Sweetie to a sapling next to Heath's horse and crept onward, guns drawn. Her gunslinger instincts prickled.

She edged inside the cave. Cold, mineral air slid in her nose and throat. She stepped quickly behind a long twisting cave pillar, her chest heaving with panicky breaths. Deliberately, just like her daddy always showed her, she calmed her breathing. She slowed her heartbeat, eased her muscles still. Focused her attention on her environment.

Slow drip-dripping of moisture. A quick scrabbling sound, like a mouse running away. Light blooming from somewhere deeper in the cave.

Should she get the sheriff?

Opal tightened her fists around her guns. Naw. He might not believe her. Or it might just take too long. Heath might need her urgently.

She edged farther into the cave, slithering from one pink twisting stalactite to a lumpen, slippery, hunched-dwarf-shaped stalagmite.

Was that a quick-indrawn breath?

Everything stilled. Opal waited. Nothing. Perhaps it was her own.

She slid behind another textured shape, and another, until she had almost reached the deep rear cave and Heath's hideout.

A tall, lean figure stood with its back to her. Not

Heath.

Squashed ten-gallon hat. Clothed in inky darkness. Yellow lantern light on the gun hand, outstretched and steady. Aiming back in there the darkness.

"Heath!" Opal called.

The dark figure whirled. A bullet cracked and echoed. The column she crouched behind shattered in a thousand glittering shards, flying through the cave.

She fell to the ground, arms covering her head as she rolled behind a lumpy stalagmite, holding her pistols clear. A short hail of bullets pinged from the twisted cave formations all around.

A wave of air as the figure rushed past. She lay on the wet cave floor, her pistol tracking the fleeing figure.

Silence.

"H-Heath?" Opal quavered, a million dread scenarios flashing in her mind.

"Opal!" Strong, welcome hands wrenched her to her feet and enclosed her in leather, sage, and heat. For a long moment, Opal held on, pressed against him, wallowing in his closeness and vitality. She pressed her cheek against his chest, let the strong beat of his heart soothe and calm her own racing blood.

"H-Heath." Hot tears sprang unbidden. "Why is the Adder after you?"

"I wish I knew. Wait here."

She ignored him, racing close on his heels to entrance of the cave, pistols drawn, and peered over his shoulder into the night. "Gone. We hope."

His burly arms wrapped around her. "Opal—you're muddy, cold, and upset. Come here, back into the cave, where I can snuggle you in blankets and give you a hot drink—and then take you back to town where you'll be

147

safe. Come on now. I'll leave this lantern here in this first cave so that dread lawman will be all lit up, if he tries to sneak back in."

She allowed Heath to take her into the cozy camp set up back in the cave, clutching him all the way.

He wrapped her tenderly in a giant tartan blanket and brewed tea on a tiny stove. He squatted down, watching her with hot eyes as she sipped her drink, welcome warmth infusing her throat and belly. "Where's the sheriff, Opal? Did you ask him to come?"

She gulped her tea. Now he was safe, a pulse of old anger spiked. "It was my opening night tonight."

Heath froze. Stood up, walked around the cave, running hands through his wild curls, already poking up in mad disarray.

He didn't reply, so she said, "Where were you?"

"Opal, you know I can't go to those places." Voice cold and hard. "I trust it went well?"

Forced politeness. Bit off words.

She threw off her rug. "An absolute, ear-ringing, total *disaster!*" Heath snapped his attention to her. "I can never go back to Wylder, never! Except to pay everyone their money back. And then I'll have to leave town, and find some tumbledown cottage far away in the wilderness where there's only coyotes and buzzards, and eke out my lonely, miserable existence until, locked with rheumatism and despair—"

"Opal." His gravel voice, and his touch, brought her to herself. "Tell me what happened." He rubbed gentle, warm hands over her shoulders and arms, with such care, as though she was a precious, miraculous being. "Tell me what you are feeling."

Opal blinked, startled. A man, asking about her

feelings?

He sensed her surprise. "Sweetheart. I know, to my cost, that bitter feelings corrode a person from the inside. Until they are just a shell, a husk, going about their daily business, with no spark of joy, no bright flashes of ideas …"

Pity for him rose in a healing wave. She drowned a lump of bitter self-recrimination in a swallow of tea. Sorted through tangles and snarls of hot and cold emotions. She was a wordsmith. Surely, she could pull out a strand…"Feeling—h-hideous, skin-peeling shame. A chest-ripping, leg-dragging, heavy conviction of utter failure. Public humiliation."

He pulled her close.

"Heath, I'm so confused. I believed, I *knew* I could do this. And now? My dream is cracked into smithereens and flown off into the wild blue yonder."

His warmth and steadiness anchored her amidst a swirling sea of raging despair. His strong heartbeat thrummed steady under her cheek. Press closer. Wallow. Cling.

He tickled her cheek. "Do you think you can describe what happened?"

She pulled away. "It all began so gloriously— Heath, it was utter magic! Your work—the old mansion transformed back into a grand dame. Proud, stately, and smiling. I thought my heart would burst from excitement and happy gratitude." She sniffed. "People queued for hours. Flooded into the theater. The lights! The noise! The chatter and music…"

"Go on."

"Are you sure? Will my talk trigger your…your darkness?" She laughed sadly. "Then there'll be two of us, and imagine if the Adder returned—"

"Opal. Calm yourself. I'm here. I'll be here as long as you need me."

The words pinged straight into Opal's damaged heart. Her spirits lifted. *I might just need you forever, Heath Rawdon.* He stared at her, eyes dark and melting in the lantern light.

"Oh!" Opal put fingers to her mouth. "Did I say that out loud?"

His lips twisted in a lop-sided grin. "As long as you need me. That's a sacred promise."

She gathered her scattered wits. "The play. It went to chaos almost from the beginning. Heath, I did so many things wrong! I let Bluebell go to her family and tried to organize everything myself. I wanted to give everybody a part, so that it was a true Wylder town play."

She traced the rasp of bristles along his jaw. "I went all breakneck. Far. Too. Hasty. With everything. My family are right about me."

A well of dark grief rose like water in a boiling pot, overflowing her brain and body. Hopelessness ran like lead in her veins.

"Opal. Shh now. Tell me about the play."

She dredged up some courage from somewhere deep inside. May as well flay herself completely. She described the bear cub, the triplets running amok, Olive Sagebrush shouting, people running after the cub and the triplets, the band playing wild dance music, the townsfolk hurling abuse and missiles, the great heavy curtain falling down on the cast until they were all a wriggling, shouting, swearing catastrophe.

A crack of laughter summoned her from the well of

despair.

"You dare laugh!" She jumped to her feet, shedding the confining blanket.

Heath's face was transformed. Gone was the surly, wary, watchful prospector. His eyes were alive with joy and laughter. White teeth shone in a giant grin. Another great belly laugh echoed around the cave. He gasped, "You know, Opal Calahan, I wish I'd seen that play." He bent over as another booming bellow burst from him.

Opal's lips twitched. She snapped her brows together in a frown in an effort to maintain her gloomy mood. But her mouth had other ideas, stretching in a responsive smile. Her belly quivered. And then she couldn't hold it in. "I suppose it was funny!"

Opal giggled. Then she let it come. She shrieked with mad laughter, bubbling and spilling over in a frothy catharsis. Emotional tears sprouted, spilling down her cheeks. Her whole body shook as she screamed and laughed, clinging to Heath as she laughed away her grief, and fear, and self-hatred.

His gentle fingers stroking her hair, the back of her neck, her shoulders calmed her. "You are not too hasty, Opal," he said.

"How can you say that?"

"You are quick-thinking, passionate, clever, determined. A pioneer, a leader, a star that people will follow. You only lack experience, Opal. And now you have a little."

She looked her puzzlement. Studied the lean planes of his face, sharper in the half darkness.

"Look at your calmness in every encounter with Marshal Adder Jackson. You know how to be a sharpshooter, so you are poised, confident, expert. You don't make mistakes. You don't shoot too early or hit the wrong target. A calmer, more calculated, seasoned, and precise gunslinger I've never met."

Silence. A big happy glow grew in Opal's chest, where minutes ago her black despair had sat like a demon in possession. "You want me to put on another play."

"If that's what you wish." He smoothed her hot brow, tracing each eyebrow with a fingertip. "I'll help you. I will rehearse those lines. I'll keep working on that Wylder Playhouse. Bluebell is back now, and she can earn her pay."

She stared at him, hope growing fresh, like bright tulips flowering amongst sodden grass in spring.

And then, as she gazed at his beautiful face, his damaged soul, he leaned in.

And kissed her.

Chapter Twelve

Heath wrapped her securely in his embrace. So warm, so large and encompassing. His good sagebrush and man smell enveloped her. His firm lips brushed hers, danced over her mouth. He pressed heat and hunger as his mouth met hers, harder now, wanting and needing.

"Opal," he groaned and pulled her closer. Her breasts pressed into his brawny chest, ridged with muscle from daily physical labor. Her right thigh squeezed between his long, sturdy legs.

His arousal prodded against her belly. He caressed the soft skin at the back of her neck with urgent fingers. Ran his hand along her neckline, fingers seeking and dipping along the front of her bodice.

Desire flew like a flame through her veins, pulsing and pooling at the apex of her thighs, pushing and rubbing against Heath's hard body.

His kiss—his warm, soft lips, mobile and seeking, met her eager mouth. As she opened her lips on a gasp, he slid a velvet tongue inside, stroking and tasting.

An appreciative groan hummed in her throat. Wherever he ran fingers and hands, her skin came alive, prickling and sizzling. Yearning filled her. Her breath came quick and fast.

He pulled her to him, lifted her in his strong arms—oh, the sensation!—and then laid her on her

153

discarded blanket. He lay next to her, sprinkling tiny kisses like petals falling on her cheeks, her nose, her brows and eyelashes. Over her dress, his fingers brushed her nipples, which instantly sprang into hard peaks of wanting.

Heat bloomed in her blood. He put both heavy, warm hands on her breasts, and she writhed under him. "Opal," he grated.

"Yes! Yes." She hardly knew what she said, or to what she agreed. She didn't care, but burned in this flaming fire.

Carefully, slowly, his gaze dark with need in the soft yellow glow of the lanterns, Heath unlaced the top of her bodice. He stared, a man dazed, as her soft white curves quivered, half released from their confines.

His hungry gaze on her skin as he unlaced her, drove sensation throbbing and pulsing in her lower belly. Her body flexed under the gentle touch of his fingers.

His hand stopped halfway down her lacing. "Yes?" More grit than word.

"Yes," she sighed on a soft exhale.

Instead of unlacing her further, he bent and kissed her like a starving man, sucking her bottom lip into his hot mouth, tracing her lips with the tip of his tongue, meeting her in a passionate kiss.

She pushed her chest into his hands, aching and burning with desire. He gazed down, eyes gleaming. Long, clever fingers unlaced another section, and another. At last, her breasts sprang free. He bent his mouth to her and breathed a stream of air over her taut, sensitive nipples. When she gave a small, unbidden shriek, he bent his mouth to one fat globe and gently sucked the tight nub.

Stars exploded in Opal's brain. "Oh! Mmmm. Yes. Oh!"

Showers of sparks ripped through her veins as he kneaded her plump bosom with eager, tender hands. She lay under his ministrations, helpless and burning, only able to moan encouragement.

A fingertip trailed up her leg, bunching her dress higher as it traversed her soft inner thigh. And then, he touched her—there! She bucked. A small, surprised shriek escaped her throat.

His fingers, his hands, caressed her body, over and under her dress. She sat up and rubbed her hands over him, fascinated with his form. His arms, bulging with muscle. His broad shoulders, sturdy back, ridged abdomen. She stroked the long planes of his legs.

He lay her back down, ran dancing fingers along her upper thighs. Began to tease and tickle at the hot, damp center of her, his fingertip tracing her sex.

"Say you want me, Opal," he rumbled.

"Yes! I want you, Heath Rawdon. Now!" she managed to gasp.

At last, he rewarded her wordless pleas and entreaties, trapping her with glinting dark eyes as he pushed a long finger inside her, moving in and out, tickling and rubbing. She writhed shamelessly around him, until an enormous wave of pleasure and satisfaction took her high and splintered all around the cave.

He held her tight against him until her heart slowed its pounding.

"Heath. You have made the worst day of my life into my best." He kissed her lightly on the lips. She struggled upright with jelly-muscles, took his manly jaw in both hands, and gave him a luscious, lingering, full smooch. "I just wish I could have been there in the worst day of your life."

"No matter. We relive our worst days over and over in our minds, trying to catch sense or meaning, find a pattern, trying to recreate and reinvent." He traced her round cheek. "All I know is this, Miss Opal Calahan. Thanks to the worst days of my life, here I am in another hemisphere altogether, holding you in my arms. The woman of my dreams."

He put her gently away from him, stood, and walked agitatedly around the cave. "But now, I must take you back to civilization, away from here! I have the most intense urge to take you. Here and now. Take you, possess you, ride with you. Understand, Opal? We must go from here. Now."

She sauntered up to him, mischief and sass all restored, thanks to the courage and compassion of one gloom-ridden prospector. "You can take me, Heath Rawdon, whenever and however you want. You have given myself back to me. My heart cleaves to you—a happy heart once more, filled with plans and enthusiasms. No other man could have done it. Your terrible experiences lent insight so you could cut my horrors off before they took hold."

She fell to her knees in front of him, pressed her face against his bulging groin. "Heath," she said into his moleskins. He jerked against her, a groan rumbling through him.

He reached down and gently pulled her to her feet until their faces were close and his breath misted her cheek. "I desire you so much, Opal Calahan. You tempt me in every way. Yet I must strike gold before I can offer for you."

"Stop that fiddleheaded nonsense!" Panic welled and skittered in her veins. "The gloomy, fatalistic play-hater has returned. Begone, I say! Bring back that lovely, gentle Heath—"

"I cannot separate the package. I want you, Opal Calahan, more than man has ever wanted a woman. But I will not offer you fools' gold, that glittering, worthless metal that gives a brief illusion of pleasure, a momentary golden moment. I must be able to give you your whole dream. To give you a safe, secure life."

Now that tolled within her like a great bell. Oh, yes.

"Don't be silly," she said instead. "There is no other man for me. There never will be."

"Come now," was all he answered. "Let me take you back to town."

At the cave entrance, he suddenly turned and held her tight. "I—adore you, Opal Calahan," he muttered into her hair.

"And I adore you, Heath Rawdon. There is nothing I would not do for you."

Heath squeezed her tight, the thrum of his steady, strong heart calling to her blood.

She could have held him all night. When he released her, she felt bereft. He said, "You don't have to learn not to be foolhardy, love. I think rather, you must trust your own excellent judgement. Not blindly accept the world's verdict of what you are. One tiny incident happens in childhood, or later, and we are branded by our families and society forever. Takes years to out-live that snap judgement—their *hasty* assessment—of our character and behavior."

Opal said nothing, but turned his words over in her mind as they caught their horses and mounted. She loved this new way of defining herself!

She had more worries. As they trotted back to Heath's camp and Wylder, Opal said, "Do you think Marshal Adder Jackson believes you have gold in that cave? And he wants to get his grubby mitts on it."

"He believes something, anyway. That's another reason I cannot offer you the world, Miss Calahan. That lawman is on my hammer night and day. I dread the future."

She rode close, reached over, and took his hand. "The only dread you need to have, Heath Rawdon, is what idiot, hasty thing I will do next."

She wrung a laugh from him, anyway.

"You are not hasty, Opal," he growled. "I told you what I think."

And her heart sang within her once more.

****

Planning. Preparation. Double-checking. Delegating. Do the work, do the work.

Heath talked her through it all, as they strolled slowly back to Wylder from his camp, bumping hips, grazing hands, twining fingers, all the way. "Exactly like setting up a mine. Your success depends on it. Your life."

"I do know all this, I suppose," Opal declared. "It's just...boring!" They both laughed.

"Learn to love the boring. Embrace the work, the fun parts and the grind. Then your play will rise phoenix-like from the ashes of your reputation, to stun all of Wylder and beyond."

They paused at the little foot bridge, tilting their heads up at the dome of stars shimmering in the inky sky above. "Star-gazing," Opal whispered. "Somehow their faraway sparkling gives me hope. New determination. I can do this. I *will* do this."

Heath placed his big hands on her shoulders and turned her to face him. "You are the most determined woman I've ever had the privilege to meet. You aren't hasty, Opal. You're calm and deliberate when need arises. You're quick-thinking, mercurial, impatient only when things move slowly. The rest of us are puffing to catch up with you. Beautiful, glorious you."

Could there be anything more seductive than a ruggedly handsome man, bristling with protective strength, telling her lovely things about herself, under a huge, starry sky?

Opal didn't think so.

She stood on tippy-toes and kissed him.

Her soft mouth met his firm lips. His warmth engulfed her. His need and hunger called to a place deep inside her. He kissed her back, passionately, a man starving for love, then pulled away. "Take you back to warmth and comfort, Miss Calahan," he rasped.

"I've got those right here," she whispered against his neck, and felt his responsive shiver on her skin. "With you."

His heavy arm clasped her against his side as they crossed the little bridge and sauntered into the light alleyways leading to bright-lit Wylder Street.

They rounded the corner and halted, Opal banging hard into Heath, who shot out a hand and caught her as she stumbled.

An enormous queue of people snaked in a zagged

line from the steps of the Vincent House Hotel, north up Wylder Street all the way to Opal's Playhouse. A shouting, cursing, milling *angry* snake.

The harassed Vincent Hotel doorman and several stocky barmen held the crowd back, shouting platitudes and warnings into the ruckus. "She ain't here!" "Come back tomorrow at a decent hour—she promised you all refunds."

Opal slammed back into the laneway, her heart thundering. "Bluebell! Is she in the hotel? I trust she is all right." She gripped Heath's muscle-ridged upper arms. "They'll throw me out of the Vincent after this latest outrage! I'll have to find somewhere else to stay. And blast it! Where am I going to find all their refunds? I must pay the cast their promised wages, and—"

Heath smoothed her hair in a distracted fashion. A heavy frown creased his brows. "You can come back to my camp for the night." Their eyes met, glimmering in the reflected streetlights leaching in from Wylder Street. A pulse of emotion hummed between them.

Whew. Yes. She'd love to stay with him. In his tent. Alone together.

Images of his clever fingers dancing over her body until she writhed and shrieked flooded her mind. Heat gathered in her skin.

He touched her jaw lightly. His fingertip burnt her skin. She might combust with desire.

A piercing whistle shattered the tension.

The sheriff and four cowboys rode across the entrance to the laneway. Heath and Opal crept forward and peered into Wylder Street. The line of cranky play-goers extended farther north. Anger simmered closer to boiling.

The sheriff and his deputies rode into the fray. The sheriff's clear voice commanded, "Everybody disperse now. Go on to your homes! Go on, git along there. Come back at a godly hour." One of his deputies raised his arm, and two gunshots split the air.

The crowd muttered and complained, but several peeled off and began heading away from the Vincent. Finally, most of the crowd fragmented and turned back into Wylder citizens.

"Maybe I better still come back to your tent?" Opal said. "They might come back."

Heath shot her a heavy-lidded, tortured look. "You'll be safe here now. Come on. Back to civilization with you."

"How about you come and tell the sheriff about the marshal? Something very wrong about that lawman. I don't want to come visit and find you missing—or worse."

Heath's mouth creased in a bitter smile. "I can look after myself. We can't tell the sheriff, now I'm back safe—hear me, Opal? Because then I'll have to reveal my hideout cave."

"But you haven't done anything wrong! You don't need a hideout cave."

"I have good reason not to trust the vagaries of the law." He snapped the words. Gave her a gentle poke in the kidney. "Quick. Get yourself inside while the sheriff's here. You'll be safe inside."

"But Heath—"

"Get." He jerked his head. She jutted her jaw up and glared at him, but his face blanked into bored impatience.

Well. Fine then.

Opal gave him a saucy look, tossed her head, and got.

She greeted the exhausted doorman, Parkinson, who met her with his usual charming courtesy, not giving away by a muscle that she'd caused a rumpus of a major magnitude. Opal sneaked a look back. The prospector was nowhere to be seen—but she felt him watching her safe inside, all the same.

What a night! If she could capture in a drama that rollercoaster of action and emotion that her life had become, her plays would sell—

"Miss Opal Calahan?" An elderly, quavering voice.

Oh, what trouble beset her now? Opal hesitated. She could sprint straight up those stairs to her room, pretend she hadn't heard. How she wanted to wash, eat a snack, and just tumble into bed.

She just couldn't deal with another thing tonight.

She wanted to lie in her warm bed, relive kissing Heath in their own private cave, retrace the sizzling touch of his fingers on her secret skin.

The voice belonged to a white-haired old dame, shakily leaning on a stick. Cheeks as wrinkled as last fall's wild apples. Dressed in ancient fashions, neat as a pin. Oh Lord. The merest gust of wind would blow her right down the Vincent front steps.

"Yes, I'm the infamous, the maligned, the disgraced Miss Opal Calahan."

The frail old thing shook with laughter, until Opal worried the biddy would lose her grip and fall down right there on the vestibule carpet. "How can I help you? Please, come and sit down in the dining parlor. I don't know that they'll serve me after tonight's debacle," she confided. "So I might have to fetch you a cup of tea or something from the bar myself."

The woman quivered all over in a melodious giggle. Such spirit and ready humor! Curiosity pricked in Opal's veins. She escorted the old lady at her snail's pace into the dining parlor and assisted her with the laborious process of sitting down on a high, hard chair.

"Shall I get you a hot drink?"

"Tea. With a wee dram added to warm me." The withered, lip-sticked mouth parted in a wicked, conspiratorial grin. Her black eyes flashed. Opal bustled away to make the tea and whiskey, fully awake now, the mystery of this elderly mischief-maker calling to her own zesty spirit.

She paused at the doorway to the bar, her heart pounding. She expected a massive dressing down and possible eviction from the respectable Vincent House Hotel. She dreaded seeing the look of disapproval and disappointment in the affable housekeeper Molly Maguire's eyes, who had been so kind to her.

There! The bar was vacant, just for a moment. Opal whipped in and poured a generous glass of amber whiskey. She crept through to the kitchen, put a finger to her lips to the sole weary kitchen maid still preparing tomorrow's victuals. Took the simmering kettle from the hob, made two cups of lovely hot tea, splashed in a generous amount of whiskey in each cup and left a dram in the glass for the now-smiling kitchen maid.

She crept back to the dining room, hoping her strange guest hadn't fallen asleep. No—she waited bright-eyed, with the impatience of those with not much time left.

The white-haired old lady took a few hefty swallows of her drink and smacked her wrinkled lips together. "A fine drop. Thank you, my darling."

"Always tastes better when it's stolen," Opal said, to make a joke. The old dame laughed. They clinked cups.

"You are a young woman who has arrived and set this town by its ears!"

Opal listened hard for clues to her new friend. Posh voice. Wealthy schooling at some stage in her life. Held herself upright, as though she'd had a backboard strapped to her in her youth, and books balanced on her head. Opal hadn't had a backboard, but her father had trained them to stand straight and exercise their muscles, so they were in full control of their bodies, their posture still and steady when needed. So that their bodies wouldn't let them down in the critical moment.

"Oh, I had my day stirring up California and the Wild West. Wylder is a rowdy place now, sure, but the frontier was a mad, bad place years ago." Her elderly new friend sighed. "How I enjoyed myself. How I dared to dream, to live flamboyant and glorious."

The lady's hand shook as she replaced the cup in its saucer, rattling the china and slopping tea on the small polished table. Opal leapt to tidy it quickly, lest her friend feel mortified.

"Thank you, my sweet. Now, where was I? Oh yes. Dare to dream. Grab this town by the whirligigs and give it a good shaking up."

Such naughty slang delivered in those plummy accents, and by a woman of advanced years, made it all sound so bad. Opal gave a most unladylike snort of laughter and collapsed in giggles.

"Miss Delphina Matilde Treadway." The woman raised her chin impressively. Peered hopefully at Opal.

Opal squinted at her, a pulse of excitement spiking. That name again. "I'm pleased to make your acquaintance, Miss Treadway. You already know my name. Miss Opal Calahan." She paused.

The old lady's face fell. "I thought a playwright might have heard of me?" Her lip-sticked old lips wobbled. Her black eyes got a little shiny.

Opal swallowed. Oh dear. "I had an unusual upbringing, ma'am. I'm not your usual playwright. I'm actually a—" Opal inhaled. Coughed. "I'm a gunslinger, ma'am."

Miss Treadway's whole face lit, and a raucous laugh tumbled out. "Better and better."

A wave of weariness caught Opal unawares. She really had to get to bed, sleep off some of this extraordinary day's worries and excitements. "I'm so pleased to have made your acquaintance, Miss Treadway. Are you staying at the Vincent? I can certainly help you with your refund, if that's why you wanted to speak with me. Hold there a moment longer, and I'll run up and get it." Opal pushed her chair out and rose.

"Refund! I don't want a refund. Sit back in your chair, girl, until I've said my piece."

"I'd be delighted, ma'am," Opal snapped back. "Tomorrow. Now, I must get to b—"

"I own that playhouse."

Had she heard right? Or had she put too much whiskey in her tea? Maybe she was so tired she had begun hearing voices. Imagining things.

Slowly, Opal folded herself back into her chair, staring at Delphina Matilde Treadway.

The old voice creaked, "That's my music hall

165

building. From my glory days." Pink spots glowed in her cheeks. "It was a trading post on the Oregon Trail. I bought it back in '45 and began transforming it into my foolish dream—a playhouse on the prairie! Folk said I was addle-headed, but often stir-crazy works just fine in show business. Besides, I could see the West was opening up."

She patted Opal's hand. "I had the stage made and installed the fancy seats and the decorations in the main theatre and the foyer. My business for later, you know? Then the California goldrush exploded, and I went there for my second stage career, entertaining those new-rich miners. I tripled my fortune and came back to Wylder later. I always dreamed of completing my biggity playhouse!"

Opal swallowed. Oh no. Now she was really in trouble. Did the old woman's friendliness mask an imminent bid for compensation? For rent? She'd be within her rights.

"I c-can't find any rent just yet. I have to give all the patrons a refund for tonight's disaster. I'm so sorry. I asked everyone—why didn't they know you owned the place? Please don't call the law down on me. How much compensation do you consider is reasonable?"

Nausea curdled in her stomach. Alarm speared her. All Heath's improvements—illegal works. Oh, blast it all to hell.

"I'm sorry," she whispered. "I'm just far...too...hasty." She put her head in her hands so Delphina didn't see the hot tears springing from burning eyes and stinging her cheeks.

A claw pulled her left hand away with surprising strength.

"You are an impetuous little thing, aren't you? Quick to judge? Wipe your eyes, child. I'm giving you the Prairie Music Hall to use for your playhouse. Rent free."

Hope snapped Opal's eyes to Delphina's face. She wasn't messing with her.

"I c-can?" And then a blaze of glory burst over her. The Wylder Playhouse! For her own use! "Bless you, Delphina Matilde Treadway. May all the stars shine on you with magic glitter. I'm not calling you Miss Treadway any longer. You are my marvelous, beautiful, generous friend Delphina Matilde—and my first successful play, coming shortly, will be written in your honor."

The woman laughed. Opal rose again, came around, and carefully hugged Delphina. Her heart absolutely overflowed with gratitude.

Her new friend and benefactor smiled all over her face and said, "I want to see the old place alive with light and laughter, glamor and glitter once more before I die. I wish you well, Miss Opal Calahan, gunslinger and playwright."

"This play will have a central role for a mature, yet sprightly female lead. Are you up for it?"

"My dear, I'd give much to walk the boards once more. I'll try not to scare all your patrons away. Now, I'm staying here at the Vincent tonight, because I hoped to speak with you, my darling. I will see you in the morning."

Dizzy with new hope, Opal walked Delphina to her room, then sped up the stairs, to be welcomed by an effusive, panicky Bluebell.

167

"Tomorrow!" Opal said, washed at bullet speed and fell into bed.

Chapter Thirteen

What was that? A blue flash in the rock face. Maybe a fluorescent beetle. Heath wiped his forehead with his sleeve, streaked with sweat and mud. He put down his heavy mattock, pushed the heels of his hands into his groaning lower back muscles. Grabbed his small hand pick from his tool belt and tapped at the rock face. Scraped, smacked, prodded. Chip, chip away.

Fair dinkum. That flash must have been his imagination. Too fired up lately, that was the trouble. That, and a new desperation powered through him. He *must* find gold. Opal needed him.

He'd planned to steadily work his claim for five years until he got the land grant. Finding gold would be a welcome bonus. But five years was too long away to be any help to Miss Opal Calahan. She needed him now, this week. Today.

He had to find gold.

There! Another flash as he turned. He clenched his fists to fight the almost overmastering urge to hoist his heaviest pick and smash the rock wall to flinders, blowing it apart in search of gold and gems. Patience. Tickle it apart as carefully as a lover. Tease her for her treasures, tempt her to give up her secrets willingly.

Nothing.

Nothing, nothing. Curse it all to hell and back.

Bloody, blasted, cursed luck.

Heath sat in the dark mine shaft, uncaring of the dirt and discomfort. What else could he do to help that lovely, feisty maiden? Think, fool!

He stared up at the square of night framed by the opening of his mine shaft. He gazed in frustration at that silver star twinkling down at him.

Silver star.

The scene from earlier tonight flashed in his mind. He leaped to his feet. His brain exploded with his sensational idea. Could he pull it off?

Silver star. He could get a job as a sheriff's deputy, just like those cowboys tonight. He could earn a regular wage, work his claim in the off-hours. He could prove to Opal, Wylder, the sheriff, and *himself*, that he was a good guy.

Heath climbed out of the shaft and walked haphazardly around his camp, talking out loud, waving his arms, rehearsing his speech to the sheriff. Counting up those attributes that made him a candidate for a deputy's badge.

Heath Rawdon was a hard man from the sewers of the goldfields. He could fight dirty or clean, shoot straight as an arrow, run and ride flat out for hours. He could stalk silently through bush or scrub, drink moonshine for hours and keep his wits.

The law wasn't well regarded back on the Victorian goldfields—Us and Them. If you lagged to the constables, you were a dog, betraying your mates, betraying your class.

He'd jump that divide for Opal Calahan. Hell, he'd walk barefoot through fire for her.

First thing tomorrow. Shaved and spruced up, clean and tidy, boots shining.

****

"You want to be my deputy." The sheriff studied him, unsmiling. He was the hardest of hard men himself. No nonsense, Heath thought. Shrewd. Straight.

"Yessir." Heath twisted his hat in his hands, frowning. "Not my usual course to ask another man for something, Sheriff. Apologize if I'm making a mull of it." He cleared his throat. The urge to flee thrummed in his blood. He stood firm. Locked eyes with the sheriff.

"I hear mighty different tales about you from Ballarat town, Mr. Heath Rawdon." The lawman waited a beat. Heath didn't say anything.

The sheriff tipped his hat back and scratched his head. "Dangerous murderer. A good bloke. An innocent man wrongly accused."

Heath raised his brows in surprise. "Someone said that?"

"Why? Are they wrong?" The sheriff's eyes narrowed to slits.

Heath huffed a laugh. "I rehearsed a speech for you, Sheriff. Why I'd be an asset to the law out here. That speech doesn't seem so shiny now. Full of holes. But I'll say it anyway. That's what I decided, so I'll do it. Only take a few minutes."

The sheriff smiled with half his face. Leaned back on the counter. "Hit me then, prospector."

Heath squinted at him. Clenched a fist, held it up. Hesitated.

The sheriff grinned with his whole face this time. "Not with your fist. With your words."

"It's crossing the line for a goldfields spawn like me to put my hand up for the law. Wild place, the Victorian goldfields. Murder, pub brawls, knife fights, fist fights, every damn kind of battle that men can do against other men. A lad must learn fast and early how to win. The rigid code of the goldfields: protect your mate. Look after those not doing so well. Mind your own business. And a lesson that came hard for me, Sheriff: don't trust the law."

The sheriff scratched his nose. No hurry. "So what are you doing here in Wylder, spouting on to me, pardner?"

Heath smiled a little. That laconic style was like goldfields culture, where a man let another man take his time. "This place is wild. Dangerous. Full of drunk, lonely cowboys, trigger-happy gunsharks. People who may not be who they pretend. I'd be happy to put my dangerous life to service."

The sheriff barked a laugh. "Yep. That's one mighty fine speech, son." His clever dark gaze sharpened. "Now cough up the real reason."

A bolt of panic slammed into Heath's chest. "You can't refuse me, Sheriff."

"So explain."

"You deputized those wild cowboys, no problems, last night."

The sheriff's brows shot into his hairline as he registered that Heath had been somewhere near the riots last night. "They are boys I know well. I understand their lengths and limits. You? You're an enigma, Mr. Heath Rawdon. Dodging and weaving my questions."

Heath cleared his throat. *Because I love Miss Opal Calahan.*

He couldn't say it. Couldn't say those shining words casually to another man. Before he'd told the woman herself. Didn't seem right.

He stood straight. Put out his hand. "The offer's there, Sheriff. When you need me."

The sheriff aligned his body to standing and shook Heath's proffered hand. "If you won't—or can't—tell me your tale, then I require a demonstration of your fitness for the law. I understand a man might have his reasons for declining to elaborate." A humorous spark lit in the depths of his dark eyes. A flash of suspicion blinded Heath—did the man know anyway?

"Sign me as your deputy." Heath hated asking another man for favors. Made his skin itch. "You can unsign me if you aren't happy."

"I'm not happy now, pardner. Can do a lot of damage signing the wrong cowboy. Corruption. Bullying. Payoffs. So git your carcass out of here, come back when you've got a story to tell, or a wanted felon under your arm. Clear?"

Heath nodded once.

He stepped to the door. Turned back. Coughed. The sheriff leaned against the counter, watching him with that shrewd gaze.

"That marshal, Adder Jackson? He's up to some malarky in the mountains. Don't like his smell."

The sheriff straightened. "If you think to ease your way in by blackening another man's reputation, that's not my way, prospector."

Denial and frustration slammed through Heath like a rock hammer. "That's not—"

"We're lucky to have Federal Marshal Adder Jackson here in Wylder."

Heath banged his way out of the small station, fuming.

That's what came of lowering yourself to ask

something of another man. Better to plough on in his own way. Be his own man.

Damn and blast that sheriff.

He resisted the urge to sneak a peek at the vibrant Opal and stalked back to his claim, cursing the stubborn lawman for putting an unexpected spoke in his wheel.

"Arrest a wanted felon." Well, he didn't have time to go chasing all over the country for criminals.

And as for telling the sheriff his real reason? Bah!

****

Molly Maguire stood barring the doorway to the breakfast room, hands on hips, jutting elbows. Far worse was the grim, determined expression on her set face.

Oh no. Opal stopped at the doorway, Bluebell bumping into her from behind. "Whoops, sorry, Miss Calahan," the girl bleated.

High spots of color danced in the housekeeper's cheeks. "This is a respectable hotel. We cannot have a repeat of the outrage last night. Riots in front of the Vincent. Patrons having to push through rabble to get through. The sheriff called to break up the crowd!"

Ice water poured down Opal's spine.

Mrs. Maguire's Irish lilt strengthened in her distress. "I'm instructed to ask you to pack and leave, Miss Calahan. The powers that be wanted to give you the heave-ho last night, but I had pity for two lone women, young as you are, I said you must be allowed your sleep. And your breakfast, but you must pack and leave and be gone from here by midmorning."

The housekeeper stood firm.

"No!" whispered Opal. Panic curdled in her stomach. Gripped her throat like a vise. "C-can you tell me which establishment might accommodate me now, Mrs. Maguire?" A terrible shaking began in her limbs. *Steady now, Opal,* her father's calm voice said in her mind. She did the breathing, her muscles slowly unbunching, her short, worthless breaths gaining depth down into her squeezing tight lungs. Loud ringing clanged in her ears. The housekeeper's lips moved, but Opal couldn't hear a thing she said. "S-sorry, Mrs. Maguire?"

"Breakfast!" hissed Bluebell from behind. "I'm hungry, can we go in?" Opal felt a firm nudge in her back. Bluebell bumping her to go into the breakfast room.

She almost laughed.

"Not Culpepper's, that's for sure," Molly Maguire said. "Listen, wee girl, why don't you go in and eat. I'll have a word. See if I can change it all to a Final Warning. Will that do you now?"

"Oh, thank you!" Grateful tears sprouted. "I'm sorry, I don't mean to cry on you, just I'm hungry and I get a little emotional if I haven't eaten..." Opal emitted a quivering laugh.

The housekeeper engulfed her in a soft, warm hug. "Get to your breakfast now. Molly will see you safe." She bequeathed a kiss on Opal's hair and propelled her into the room, redolent with toasted bread, eggs and ham, fried beans, and other wonders.

"Thank you!" Opal called after her retreating form. She and Bluebell seated themselves decorously in the breakfast room, then launched into several helpings of hot buttery toast, scrambled eggs and bacon, beans, fried greens, and grits with the wolfish enthusiasm of those suspecting this meal might be their last for a good while.

At last, Bluebell sighed happily. She met Opal's gaze over the table. "I mean to be a good assistant to you, Miss Opal. Now that we have a good breakfast inside to fortify us, we're a-gonna go upstairs and list all the broken pieces of our play disaster—and make a goodly long list of actions we need to take next."

Opal put down her fork and blinked at her assistant, a slow, glad smile creeping over her face. "Why, Bluebell! That's a marvelous idea. And sorry as I am to embroil you in my scrapes, I do appreciate having another woman to solve things with."

Bluebell glowed with the praise, her bright blue eyes shining with determination.

A pang of gratitude that she'd intervened in this girl's fate smote Opal. She hadn't done it with any intention except to wrest Bluebell from a choice of two equally horrible fates. And now Bluebell might be the saving of her.

Upstairs, they made a list:

* Add up available funds

* Calculate tickets sold and refunds due

* Pay refund to all the playgoers

(Add up how much money, if any, is left, Opal added mentally.)

* Review use of playhouse—confirm the marvelous Delphina Matilde Treadway's offer

* Find cheaper lodgings

* Write new play

* Never give up

"Did you hear where the bear cub went?" Opal asked.

Bluebell shrugged. "Just disappeared. Another

strange story for the Wylder Playhouse!" They added another line:

* Check neighborhood for stray bear cubs

Immensely cheered by this list, Opal slapped palms with Bluebell. She silently prayed that she would not have to tell her assistant in the near future that the money was gone and they both must return to their homes and their dread fates.

****

Time to gird her withers and face the length of the refund line—and check that the poor doorman was not being subjected to abuse and vitriol by unhappy playgoers.

How strange. A grin danced on Parkinson's features as she stepped through the great front door. She blinked.

A few dudes, mothers, and children in a tiny queue. Hardly anyone! Too early maybe. A small jostling mob clustered around the Vincent's left-hand wall, one cowboy slowly drawling out the syllables for the waiting crowd.

She strained her ears to listen. *What*?

Opal muscled through the crowd. Stared open-mouthed at the poster plastered to the hotel's imposing white wall:

To all Ticket-holders to the Play
The Gunslinger and the Rose
Your choice
Keep your Ticket, Ensure your Seat
for the Revised sell-out Stageshow
Coming soon!
Or claim your Refund from

177

Miss Opal Calahan, Playwright
The Vincent House Hotel

"Well, ah'm takin' my chances. Shapin' up to a dang good play, last time. Can't help what bear cubs take inter their heads to do. Nor them kiddles. Hevn't laughed so much in years."

Murmurs of agreement. Nods. That mob was replaced by the next crowd, and the head nodding and murmurs were repeated.

Opal beckoned the short queue for refunds inside and instructed the front desk to issue payments and notes, which she would make up from her paltry funds.

Back outside, she tapped her feet and rubbed her hands on her skirts, nervously awaiting developments. Parkinson told her that the sheriff and his deputies had made fifteen arrests, and a visiting surgeon had stayed up nearly all night attending to injuries and ailments, shocks and smashes directly caused by her play debacle.

Oh no! Opal slapped a hand over her mouth. How kind of the surgeon. She'd have to check if he'd been paid too.

Her eyes widened in her head. The urge to flee tingled in her legs and feet. The Sagebrush family were heading straight up the road toward her, a mini-tornado of action and noise: triplets running riot, Olive hollering, and Nartan dad-bellowing. Opal forced herself to calm and stand firm. What trouble lay in store now?

"I'm so sorry!" Opal called as the family neared the Vincent. The doorman frowned, but she placed a hand on his arm. "Is your son all right? Taken no harm from last night?" She waited, trying to slow her panicky breathing.

"We've come to apologize, Miss Calahan," Olive Sagebrush hollered. "Our Terrible Triplets don't mean any harm. They're just healthy, curious boys, testing their limits. But they can sure cause havoc!"

Opal ran down the steps and hugged Olive. "Not at all! You couldn't help the excited bear cub. I don't know where the creature came from, and it vanished again." The leather-tanner Nartan pulled one of the triplets close and stood tall, glowering and protective.

"In fact," Opal babbled, "I'm writing a new play, and my assistant has returned, so it should all run far more smoothly this time with her help, and I'd love to have you all acting in it, if you care to?"

Olive Sagebrush laughed. "You're a one." She patted Opal's chest, over her heart. "Brave and true. Come and visit with us, when you have a chance?"

Opal nodded, delighted, and waved as the Sagebrush family hurricane headed off down Wylder Street.

Ten minutes later, Opal sat stunned and delighted in the breakfast room with a sustaining cup of tea. Bluebell chirped in excitement, making a whole new list entitled "Stage Show Two—Assistant Duties."

Molly Maguire bustled in. Opal leaped up and embraced the kindly housekeeper, who announced, "You have the honorable Miss Delphina Matilde Treadway to thank for your change in fortune. She's cleared a path through your disaster like an old-fashioned, courteous, irresistible oxen train."

Opal laughed. She raised her brows and waited.

"Seems she rose early and tottered off to the

newspaper office and arranged for the printing and distribution of a wagon-load of pamphlets, plus the poster on the front wall."

"It's very good of the Vincent to allow a large poster plastered over their front wall."

"You're one of our own now, Miss Opal. I'm sure one day we'll be boasting you wrote your first play while you stayed here." Molly grinned. "And Miss Delphina is a hard lady to say no to."

So far, she'd issued five refunds. Only five! Seemed like a miracle after her all-encompassing disaster that had erupted like a rioting volcano all over Wylder.

The lady of the hour, Miss Delphina Matilde Treadway, wobbled in unsteadily with her cane, two pink spots high in her cheeks. Opal rushed to ease her into a chair. Her elderly friend appeared both exhausted and elated. She held up a be-ringed, veined hand, still pale and white from a lifetime of wearing gloves. "Shh, child. Let me get my breath. Go and order me a cup of tea, if you will—with a good dash of whiskey to warm my old bones."

Her friend clasped shaking hands around the warm cup. "I've given an interview to the newspaper. That man's been pestering me for years. I called the play a riotous success and talked up your skills, my dear. There'll be a special afternoon print edition, and it will hit the streets in a matter of hours. Everyone's been promised a new play, for next Saturday."

Hot, happy tears sprang to Opal's eyes. "I don't know how to thank you!"

"Bring my music hall back to glowing, glittering life. That will be thanks enough."

Opal knelt before her friend and took her hands. "I mean it about the...*mature* female lead. We'll turn the usual practice on its head!" She rose and paced around the room. "Together we'll show them! Getting on in years don't mean sittin' by the fire and knittin'! Oh no! You'll be striding the boards again soon, Miss Treadway, Delphina Matilde. You'll be an inspiration to every woman who wants to grow old full of courage and action!"

"That's the spirit. Now, my darling, would you walk with me to the street, where my carriage is waiting? After all the excitement, I need a little quiet time."

"I'll go and call it for you now, ma'am. I'll bring it right to the door of the Vincent."

After Opal saw to her friend's needs, she danced around the empty breakfast room, waving her fists in triumph. All was not lost! Thanks to the good, generous hearts of the Wylder folk, she could keep on with her dream. She would succeed! She must. Not only did she have herself and Bluebell to support, and her youngest brother, due to arrive soon, she must meet—exceed— the expectations of the whole of Wylder, who had given her another chance.

A vision of a tall, dark-eyed prospector floated into her mind.

She must share this news with him. He'd promised to help her—and if her plan worked, it would help him too.

He would remember his love for theater and illusion. He'd recover his lost ability for pleasure and enjoyment.

And finally, he'd find the space to forgive himself.

So much ginger crackled and fizzed in her veins, she had to go and see him, now.

Chapter Fourteen

Opal headed down the back lanes toward the footbridge, hiding in the shadows a little, not too keen to bump into any irate playgoers.

Halfway down Sidewinder Lane, her steps slowed. What did she know about Heath? A loner, yes, a self-sufficient, determined, obsessed man—and a *kind* man. She swiveled and hurried back toward Wylder Street and the new Wylder Playhouse.

She burst in the front entrance, shoving down horrible recollections of the mayhem last night.

And there he was.

"Heath! Such news!"

How her stupid heart beat as his dark gaze lit as he set on eyes on her. How her silly stomach did loop-the-loops as she regarded him, his tall, muscular frame balanced high on a makeshift scaffold, hammering and repairing, *just for her*.

He brushed dark curls, damp with sweat, from his forehead and put down his tools. Climbed down the scaffolding, lithe as a panther, sending her foolish heart smashing beneath her ribs and robbing her breath.

Magnificent. Strong. So taciturn, yet so responsive to her, so magnetized by her presence. Holy moly, did that self-contained man's lean cheeks redden as he strode toward her?

"Opal." Her name on his expressive mouth,

183

normally a hard line of determination, but soft and wanting now. He took her shoulders in his big, warm hands. "Are you well?" He studied her expression. He traced her cheekbone, the line of her jaw with two long fingers.

She inhaled his scent. His usual sage and leather, mixed with fresh sawdust with a whiff of metallic, oiled tools. She preened under his stroking, savoring his touch.

"I've met the owner! A vibrant, hilarious old dame called Miss Delphina Mathilde Treadway, and that wonderful woman saved my sorry hide from a public flaying. *And* stopped the Vincent from heaving me and Bluebell out onto the street."

Heath brushed his fingers down her face. He cupped the back of her head in his large hand. "Opal! That's tremendous! Stupendous. I'm so happy for you."

"She used to tread the boards, right here, singing and dancing, and got so famous she ended up owning the place. So my revised play will have a pivotal part for one sprightly, talented heroine, never mind about being in her seventies. Or eighties."

Opal smiled up at him. "This time, Heath Rawdon, you will practice those lines with me. So I can hear how they sound. Make adjustments."

Heath stared down at her, a complex wave of emotions chasing each other over his face. Then his lips firmed, and his dark eyes blazed in resolution.

"That's right," Opal encouraged, soft-voiced. "I need you, Heath. My play last night, excited as I was, seemed like a half a play without you. I kept looking for you so I could share the magic and excitement. Even if you'd sat far at the back, near the exit—just seeing you there, would have—" She swallowed.

He waited, one hand smoothing her upper arm. Lord, that felt heavenly!

"I have courage, and I have daring and gall, all that stuff, but I need my anchor, my lodestone, my compass. That feels mighty like you, Heath Rawdon. My whole being swivels toward you when you enter the room. I sense you out there under the stars, my own private star, giving me hope and boosting my courage and leading my way."

His cheeks bunched. His voice emerged in a gritty rasp. "I suppose—hmm. I suppose that's one of your characters speaking?"

Her blood leapt to deny his doubt, to claim the words. They tumbled out, quick and urgent. "No, Heath. This is me, Opal Calahan, woman to man. This is how I feel about you."

He didn't hear her. His deep voice rumbled over hers as she spoke. "Here's a character for you. You can have this one for free. Picture this. A lonely prospector, picking out the years until he can make a land claim. Wants nothing more than a five-acre piece of earth he can call his own. To rest his weary, plaguey bones, find some peace. And then a flower blooms suddenly from the arid desert earth, a flower so unlikely, so sweet and beautiful, he wonders if he's died and gone to heaven.

"I love you, Opal Calahan. I love you with every atom of my being, with everything I've got to give. When you are with me, sweet golden angels blow victory trumpets in my ear, my black and withered heart heals pink and sings for glory. My blood hammers and longs for you, my skin yearns to slide against yours, my mind craves your company, your voice, your ideas.

"I don't care what I've done, what I've been. Everything is made new with you."

Opal stood, his words spinning in her brain. A great wave of happiness spilled through her. "Heath," she whispered, and then his face lowered and his firm lips brushed hers, softly asking, then demanding, claiming her.

His strong arms came around her, pressing her close to him. His heart thudded steady and strong into her outspread fingers. "Opal," he groaned. "You mustn't fall for a larrikin like me. You'll waste yourself."

"Heath Rawdon! How can I waste myself when you've guided me and protected me, accepted me in all my quirks and foibles? Encouraged me in my outlandish schemes and dreams, until they seem not only possible but you help make them come alive? You are the man for me. My heart and mind say so, my skin burns for you—and my nose especially informs that you are my man!"

A deep rumble of laughter. "Your nose? No—don't explain. I understand. My nose wants to bury himself in your hair, your skin, your..." He coughed.

"My?"

"One day, soon, I'll show you how my nose wants to smell you all over. You are a playwright. Let the story unfold in the right time, scene by scene, experience by experience."

"Now you are teasing me!" Opal ran her fingertips along his bristly jaw, enjoying the rasp. "Words do have their own magic." She gazed into his lovely dark eyes, so expressive, old pain almost alchemized into fierce, passionate joy. "You could describe what your

186

nose wishes to discover, then I'll have something to replay, to imagine, deep in the black night, when I'm alone in my bed."

His eyes blazed. A thunderous growl made her toes curl in her boots and her heart spike. "Opal." The single word held a warning note.

Mischief rose in her. "Show me now, my Heathcliff." She looked around. "There's nobody else here."

"They could venture in at any moment. Some gunslinging cowboy."

"Adds a little spice, don't you think?"

He growled again and crushed her to him. "Opal, my Opal." His warm, firm lips descended on hers. He kissed her deeply, kissed her until she was dizzy and her legs felt boneless and unsteady. Delight fizzed in her veins; blood rocketed under her skin.

His left arm held her upright and steady, while his right hand began to explore the shape of her, tracing the curve of her waist and hip and the soft roundness of her bottom. Her whole body melted under his touch. Her heart hammered now, her skin cried out for his touch, her nipples strained to his solid warmth, swelling heat hummed in her feminine parts.

Then he unlocked his lips from hers and plunged his nose into her hair, sprinkling gentle, light kisses under her ear. He held her upright as he slithered down her body. Staring at her chest, making her squirm and wiggle, he carefully unlaced the top two laces, then pushed his face into the soft white skin bared there. A gasp escaped her; her breath hitched.

His face burrowing into her bodice, he breathed in noisily, murmuring, "Mmm, flowers and sunshine and warm woman."

Something was happening down below. She was all soft and warm and melting, desire beating in a thick pulse. She put out a tentative hand on his muscular shoulder. Slid it over his neck and over his dark hair, tied back in a short queue. Traced the breadth of his shoulders with both hands as she pushed her body into his face. "Unlace more," she said, demanding, imperious. Desperate.

He slid a glance up at her, his eyes wide and dark, redolent with greed and hunger. "I'd be delighted," he grated, and suited the action to the words.

Opal still stood before him, her chest heaving now as he slowly unlaced one, two, three, four laces. Oh, she would die with wanting!

He hefted deft fingers under each breast and bared her to the air, bouncing out, nipples already peaking into pink buds. He lowered his face onto her left breast and traced a path with the tip of his tongue around her nipple. "Oh, Heath! Oh. Oh." He bounced her bosoms in his hands, murmuring appreciation and admiration. Then he put his warm lips on her nipple and sucked, hard and fast. Opal almost shot to the roof, crying out in a kind of agony of delight. She pressed his head harder against her body, willing him to do it again. And again.

Her entire body writhed under his ministrations. Her brain flew off somewhere into the skies. His rasping phrases, his deep rumbling voice sent her into a greater fever of desire.

"Heath, I need...I want..."

"Yes, my desert jewel?"

"Well, actually I don't know. But you can show me. Didn't you want to inhale me?"

Heath stood. "One day, my lovely flower, I will inhale you all over. Every secret place. But that day is not today, not here." He haphazardly relaced her bodice, giving her soft kisses. "Time I returned to prospecting. I must make a claim, to fund your dreams, my Opal."

"No, you don't. We'll be fine. I can...I can take a job if I must."

"You refer to a gunslinging job. Where you could be wounded, maimed, hurt, damaged. *Killed.*"

"Not me, cowboy. I was taught by the best."

"Opal, everybody meets their nemesis. It's the way of things. Everybody. Give me time—a week, two weeks—to find something out there. All the signs are there. Just a little longer. Don't sign up for a gunfight. Please." He kissed her. All her determination melted under the force of his will. She struggled. Couldn't help herself.

"Yes, Heath," she said, and smiled at him, stars bursting in her vision in the magical moment. "I'll see you at your camp for rehearsals, soon."

He frowned and visibly battled with himself. "Yes. About that. I think you better bring Bluebell when you come. A chaperone."

Disappointment washed Opal like a bucket of water from the Medicine Bow River. Then mischief danced. "Why, Heath?" She batted her eyelashes as demurely as she knew how.

Heath closed his eyes and inhaled deeply. Opal noted with interest his clenched fists, white-knuckled as he sought self-mastery. "No, my sweet temptress. I cannot trust myself not to..."

"Yes, Heathcliff?" She said it breathily, leaning in

invitingly.

"Opal, you wanton," he groaned. "I'm well suited to Heathcliff, or Heathrod or more like caber pole right at the moment." He gestured to the front of his trousers, which indeed strained outward with a rod of enormous size.

Opal's eyes widened, and her mouth opened. She sensed she played with fire. Here was a passionate man. A deprived man. A strong, forceful, dangerous man— and she the object of his burning desire.

She shivered, pleasurably.

He picked up his hat where it had fallen, unwanted, dusted it off, and replaced it on his head. "I'll see you at the camp for rehearsal, with Miss Bluebell, mind."

"Oh, that will just bore her. She has plenty to do."

Heath raised a dark eyebrow. "I'll be packing any baggage who comes alone smartly back to town."

Opal stepped close, treated him to her best sharky glare. "I'm very glad to hear it. Lucky then, that I'm no baggage, Mr. Rawdon."

His laugh rumbled around the old music hall. He grabbed her, bequeathed a last soft kiss on her lips, tipped his hat to her, and strode toward the exit.

She watched as daylight streamed in like a stage floodlight as he opened and closed the heavy front door.

Opal's legs finally gave way, and she folded down into a dazed, happy heap.

She shut her eyes and relived those precious, exciting, incredible minutes.

Heath Rawdon had told her he loved her.

And his kiss. *Crikey!*

****

Heath pulled his hat low and slid along the

190

shadows in the narrower alleyways. It was bright day, much later than his usual departure time from the playhouse. Generally, he worked on the playhouse at night and then returned to his claim for a short sleep, then hitting the hard labor of prospecting.

Opal Calahan. How had she come into his life? Like an angel. A goddess. In the playhouse, he'd almost taken her. The desire had beat so hard in his veins, in his brain, in his cock, he'd almost exploded.

He had to find gold. He must clear his name. Then he could marry her.

His head rang with plans, interspersed with flashes of the glorious Opal. Her soft white breasts quivering and joggling in his hands, under his tongue. He groaned aloud and stopped to bend over. Imagined cold water, mud, the mine, until his huge erection subsided sufficiently to walk once more.

He barely registered his surroundings until he arrived back at his claim.

His brain cleared. Someone had been here, poking around. That blasted marshal, no doubt. What did the man want with him? To rob him, or worse. All his instincts for self-preservation screamed.

He ate a rushed breakfast and grabbed his tools. He'd sleep later. If he went to bed, visions of the glorious Opal would torment him. He may as well use that physical frustration to power his digging.

****

Two days had skittered and dawdled past.

Heath had existed in a fever of impatience to see her again, got almost a permanent crick in his neck from peering down the path toward Wylder. He'd worked his claim by day, hammered and sawed in the old mansion half the night. Waiting for his woman to claim him.

He was about to explode, on the verge of downing tools and heading into town on any flimsy pretext—groceries, music, a card game with the cowboys, when he saw her slight figure dancing down the path toward his camp.

Sun sparked on her frizzy hair, and a blue bonnet swung in her hand. The yellow gingham dress covered her slender form today, as she stepped with her customary spring and zest. Such feelings engulfed him! A glow that began somewhere deep inside. A thaw. A mad happiness, just to see her coming for him.

He threw down his tools—enough of staring like a dazzled yellow-crested cockatoo! He brushed mud off as he hastened to the creek, splashed his face, wet down his hair, scrubbed his hands, rubbed more crusted dirt from his clothes with a bunch of sagebrush and used his handkerchief to rub some shine into his old boots.

He straightened his apparel and his spine and marched into camp just as Opal appeared and folded her in his arms. The fresh cotton, flower smell of her! "I told you not to come alone!" he rumbled into her hair.

"And I didn't!" Opal stepped back, turned her head and smiled, waving someone on.

A skinny girl trotted into the camp, more big blue eyes and attitude than anything solid about her.

Heath struggled manfully with the most crashing disappointment to beset him since his gold seam turned to clay and granite. "Well. Good." The words gritted in his throat and fell like gravel.

He'd frightened Opal's assistant. Opal herself wasn't cowed by his frown. Her eyes glittered with amusement, soft like a woman's hand stroking his forehead.

He tried again, consciously softening his glower, forcing an airy tone. "Welcome to my camp. Bluebell, I believe?" He stuck out his hand.

The girl rallied, grinned like an urchin, and shook.

Worse was to come. He had to act the hero's lines—but with Bluebell. There would be no romantic scenes enacted with the lovely Opal today. Frustration tightened his jaw and thighs as they strode into the desert.

"Everything is fabulous!" Opal told him, walking next to him, brushing her hand against his. "I've only issued seven more refunds—everyone else is waiting for Saturday's new play!"

She turned her brilliant sea-turquoise gaze on him, summoning the blood rushing around his body, making him jump with life, as he hadn't for two long dreary, hopeless days.

"Rehearsals are going brilliantly—Buck Standish has most kindly agreed to be my leading man—"

Heath repressed a savage pang of jealousy and "accidentally" bumped his hip gently into hers. She wasn't fooled for a second but treated him to a saucy look that sent hot blood rushing straight to his groin. He may have groaned aloud.

"Pardon?" She treated him to a wicked smile.

"Nothing," he growled. "Rehearsals?"

"All the cast are assembled, Miss Delphina Mathilde is in her element—she is teaching me *so much* I never knew about show business…"

They found a suitable cleared patch in the sagebrush, the mountains glowing pink and purple as a backdrop, the great wide sky pale celestial blue, a single mountain eagle hovering high above.

A sudden surge of happiness flowed through Heath. Opal was here and smiling at him. All was right with the world. He smiled back. If she wanted him to rehearse lines with this skinny child, then he'd do so.

Opal arranged them. "I need to watch—see if it works. Then I might play the heroine's part, to feel what she might feel." Oho! The day got brighter.

He was deep in a dramatic scene, actually beginning to enjoy himself, trying to focus on Bluebell and not constantly sneak looks at his peremptory play director, when his quick ears picked up a horse's hooves.

He slanted a look—a long black shadow mounted on a tall horse. The figure sucked in all the light like a gloomy gray pall blanketing the bright day.

Curse that Marshal Adder Jackson, come to plague him, right at this glorious moment.

He muttered, "Excuse me," to the divas and strode back to his camp, to halt the man before he damaged property or harassed the women.

Opal and Bluebell hurried behind him.

"What do you want? Even a lawman needs permission to enter private property."

The Adder smirked, his thin lips twisting in a sinister curl. "Not if we have grounds to suspect mal*feas*ance." He drawled out the words, hissing on the esses.

Despite himself, Heath shivered. He registered a squeak somewhere behind him. A clatter. Dull thud. He kept his gaze locked with the cold snake-eyes. "Come back to trade what passes for witticisms another day, won't you. I've got visitors."

"Visitors? Where's the others?"

Heath snapped a glance around. Opal stood, color like red flags of temper burning in each cheek, eyes flashing fire. *What a woman.* He wasted a moment, gazing, entirely and utterly dazzled, at her glory. She fixed a furious gaze on the federal man. Oh no, Opal.

He jerked his attention back to the Adder. "Just an expression, Jackson. Good day. I trust you'll be on your way, now you've checked on my welfare."

"You'll call me marshal." The man directed a venomous stare at Opal. Heath stepped forward, chest out, blocking his view of her, mentally clocking the location of his sharpest tools. The lawman had one gun in his holster. No doubt she was packing pistols in her dress.

The lawman snarled, "Miss Calahan. Thought I told you to stay in town?"

"Suggested, I think might be the better term, Marshal," said Opal sweetly. *Where the hell was Bluebell?* What were the women up to? Pretending to survey his camp, he cast a quick look around for the girl. Not a sign.

"I'm a playwright, sir. In fact, I'm looking for a lawman to be in my play."

A medley of expressions danced over the Adder's leathery features. Pride. Gratification. Fear. Heath felt a surprising pang of sympathy. He knew just how that hard man felt.

Opal came forward and strutted around the lawman, much like she'd done to him that first day. "Hmm. Yes, I think you'll do well, Marshal."

The marshal visibly collected himself. Ground out,

"Ask the damned sheriff," tipped his hat to her, and rode off in a panicky flurry of dust toward the Medicine Bow Mountains.

Shared laughter felt good. He gave Opal a quick hug, then forced himself to release her. "Where's your friend got to?"

"I think she fell down your mine."

"*What?*" he scrambled to his mine, to be confronted by a muddy, bedraggled, woebegone spectacle, clinging to the ladder, and peering up at him.

"Blast it all! I mean, *crikey*. I forgot to seal the mine when I saw you women arrive—"

"Has he gone?" Bluebell quavered.

Heath climbed down and helped the trembling girl up and out of the hole.

"What got into you, Bluebell? I thought you had more spine. That old marshal's scary, sure, but we chased him away. I expect more brio from my first assistant."

"I'm so sorry, miss. But he's...he's..." Bluebell burst into tears.

Opal folded the girl into her arms, making exaggerated puzzled faces at Heath. He shrugged and went to make tea. A tough Australian prospector was the last person to know what to do with a crying woman.

"He's the man," the girl whimpered into Opal's chest.

Bloody hell. Maybe he should try bursting into tears himself. Worth it, to be squashed into those soft, welcoming, creamy globes with their pink buds. Hell. He bent over. *Freezing mountain stream, mine mud, Adder Jackson...* That worked. Rod subsided, he was able to straighten, brand new cups brimming with hot tea gripped in each hand. *Don't think about her naked tits...*

"He's the black devil hammers my ma for protection money—and worse. He's the one wants to force hisself on me, for late rent payment. He been eyeing my next sister too, but when I went home for the little one's birthday, Ma said he'd left them alone for a bit. Hadn't seen his ugly face around. Is he *here*? Has he follered me to *Wylder*?"

"That marshal is the man who's been harassing your family?" Opal turned a horrified gaze on Heath.

"Yes, miss, and when I saw him, I was so frightened I hid down that dirty mine."

"We have to inform the sheriff," Opal urged him.

"I tried already, Miss Calahan." Bitterness stung the back of his mouth. "Sheriff says Adder Jackson's reputation precedes him. Known as a hero, and murderer-catcher and thief-taker all over the west. He says we're lucky to have him out here."

"I'll take Bluebell to talk to the sheriff."

"You can try. The Adder's got such a standing in law circles that I doubt the sheriff can see the real man for the bright, glowing halo beaming out his rear end."

Heath regarded the frightened filly, still held loosely in Opal's arms. "Is it possible you've made a mistake, Miss Bluebell? You only saw him for a moment. That's very bad behavior for a lawman, specially one with the marshal's reputation. I thought he only acts tough around me as he believes I'm a criminal."

Bluebell's teary eyes widened. She bleated, "That's the man! Do you think I'd mistake him?"

197

Opal said, "That man is evil. Bluebell's testimony proves it. We can't let him run you out of town, Heath!"

"I've no intention of letting him. Stay out of his way, Miss Opal Calahan, gunslinger and playwright."

She tossed her beautiful, frizzy head. "I'll be fine."

She smiled at him, and like always, his world turned upside down.

Chapter Fifteen

Opal peered into the darkness of the theater. He wasn't here. After all his fine words. After all his promises.

Her Friday dress rehearsal for her play—the properly planned and organized one—had begun, and strain her eyes as she might, there was no tall, black-mustached, curly-headed prospector in the audience.

So much for love.

He'd just wanted to seduce her after all.

Bitterness welled inside her. You fool, Opal Calahan. You brash, ill-considered, romantic idiot of a woman. *Hasty*, Burnley's voice rang in her mind. *Hasty*.

She was almost at her long-awaited moment of triumph, and she wanted to cry. Tears trembled in her throat and stung hot and pricking behind her eyes. Hurt squeezed her stomach until she thought she'd vomit.

Opal sucked all that emotion, all her grief and betrayal deep inside.

With a huge effort of will, she focused instead on Miss Delphina Mathilde. Look at her! She'd not forgotten how to command a stage. You didn't see her age or infirmity—no, you saw a bold, brave queen of the theater, drawing you into her spell.

Opal found a smile and forced herself not to stare into the audience again. Whoops. Why wouldn't her eyes listen? *He's not here*. All right, check one more time.

A space where there should be the man of her heart.

The door slammed open. Opal hurried back from the wings and down the dark passageway. She caught the street urchin by the collar before he wrecked this rehearsal too. She'd be a laughing stock. They'd kick her out of the Vincent House Hotel for good.

It was all Heath Rawdon's fault, she thought obscurely.

"Miss Calahan! Miss Molly in the Vincent sent me to tells ya."

"Yes?" She tapped her foot.

"Ya knows how the Vincent fronts near the sheriff station?"

An uneasy suspicion snaked in her stomach and bit into her innards. She held both hands so she didn't shake the child to hurry up. She chewed on her bottom lip, welcoming the sharp shock of pain.

"That Adder Jackson done arrested the prospector out in the Medicine Bow—"

Opal searched in her skirts for a coin and flipped it to the child.

"The federal marshal locked that prospector up good. He's gonna face trial for *murder*!" the child added with relish.

She ran down the dimly lit corridor and burst into the bright, dusty, noisy street. The world clamored around her in male shouts, whinnying horses, and the crunch of wheels. *Hasty, hasty, hasty*, shrilled like a train whistle in her mind.

"Not hasty!" Opal stopped. "Mr. Heath Rawdon

calls me quick thinking, responsive, passionate. If I'm hasty, then I own it! I'm gonna *hastily* break Heath out of that rotten lockup. I'm gonna *hastily* incapacitate that evil, snake-eyed marshal." She broke into a run down Wylder Street.

She reached the sheriff's office, heaving breath into her lungs. She pulled her pistols from her skirts and fired into the air. *Bang! Bang!*

The whole street stopped what they were doing, and all eyes swiveled to her.

"A man has been wrongfully arrested for a crime he didn't do, in another jurisdiction. Mr. Heath Rawdon is comin' outa that there jail right now, and nobody's gonna stop me, you hear?"

Two cowboys pulled their guns and pointed them at her. She held her right arm high and let off another shot. "I'm Opal Calahan, one of the famous gunslinging Calahans, and I'm the best of the lot, you hear me? I'm also very *hasty*, and I'm getting my man out right now."

She fired a shot into one cowboy's hat. He gave a high-pitched terrified screech and tore off down Wylder Street. Five other cowboys threw themselves flat to the road and rolled away in dark laneways. Women screamed and pulled children after them in a stampede. Horses reared, and two carriages collided in a splintering thud. The passengers disembarked and ran crouching into Sidewinder Alley.

The actors and audience from the dress rehearsal streamed out from the playhouse into the east end of Wylder Street and gaped from a safe distance.

Opal fired another shot. Everyone left ducked for cover. Good. In case there was a gun fight, all the citizenry were safe. Hasty? Hah! Nobody was as clean and quick-thinking as she. She felt it now, all her fizzing energy distilling into her calm center, just like her daddy taught her. As though time slowed, all action, all speech, giving her all the time in the world to assess, to take action, to respond.

A tall dark shadow emerged from the sheriff's office. Adder Jackson. She pinged off a quick warning shot and took cover down the alley between the sheriff's office and the newspaper works. A shot smacked around her feet. Silence sang.

That cold voice slithered closer to where she hid. "I knew you for a gunslinger, Calahan. I will destroy your whole family." His voice stopped. She strained her ears in the unnatural hush. A women's voice shrieked from the Vincent, "*He's coming, Miss Opal!*"

Everything in Opal stilled. She inhaled, steadied herself, took one step around the corner. She fired a single shot, ducked back. Listened to the ricochet echoing off the buildings.

A grunt.

Clatter of boots. Around the back of the station. Opal crept down the narrow alley, gun first. Nothing.

She took a peek.

Opal lowered her pistol.

A silhouette showed against the mountains: a tall dark shape on a horse, bolting for the hills.

She pulled the door of the sheriff's office. No sheriff. No wonder that dread marshal could pull his stunt. No doubt he was away now to ransack Heath's claim while the goldminer couldn't protect it. She pulled drawers and open cupboards. No key, neither.

She headed to the internal door to the jail and shot the lock off.

She slammed inside and called, "Heath. Stand flat against the wall. I'm shootin' off the cell lock." The noise exploded in the space.

Then she fell into two strong, waiting arms.

"Heath," she said at last. "Meet hasty Opal Calahan, gunslinger. So proud right at this moment that I am hasty. I had to spring you, Heath. Something's very wrong with that lawman."

He smoothed her forehead, her cheeks, her shoulders and arms.

"Not hasty, my darling Opal. Smart, sassy, quick as a whip, and as brave as the Eureka Rebellion. Thank all the powers of land and sea that you are. I agree about that lawman. Now, let's get after that Adder Jackson, and resolve this once and for all."

He kissed her lightly. "Got enough bullets?"

"It's me, Heath. Course I got bullets."

And at last she found a smile.

****

Heath hustled Opal to the rear of the sheriff's office and deftly saddled two of the lawman's steeds. He boosted Opal into her saddle and swung onto his own mount. He stroked the beast's neck. "That canyon pass. He's up to something. I've tracked him a couple of times now, think I know where he heads."

"He's at your camp, Heath. He thinks you've struck gold. He'll be there, trying to find your stash of riches."

"Camp first, then mountains. It's going to have to be you to cover my back, Opal. The sheriff doesn't believe me. I don't know any cowboys well enough to know who to trust."

"Hey! You couldn't have chosen a better partner,

skirts or no skirts."

He surveyed his rescuer. "I'm inclined to agree, Opal Calahan."

And despite the danger and urgency, they smiled foolishly at each other for several long beats.

He furrowed his brow and explained, "Opal. I must catch that marshal in a felony now, or we will both be in the lock up. You understand? If you help me in this, and we fail, we'll have to flee over the mountains, to somewhere else. But me? I'm tired of fleeing. This is my final stand."

Red flushed her cheeks. "Heath!" she breathed. "You made me see it. I was always fleeing from what my family, what the world called me. I *let* them define me. Stupid! I spent years fleeing from myself—from hasty, mercurial Opal Calahan. Today, to spring you, I embraced that part of me. I no longer care. Somehow, breaking you out, I freed myself. Whether it's foolhardy, or fast-draw Calahan, that's me. I'm never gonna feel bad about it again."

Heath rode his horse close, grabbed her, and kissed her thoroughly. "After tonight...I may never get another chance to say this. I adore you, my fierce, whip-smart, passionate, *glorious* woman. You go all out for who and what you care about, and the consequences can go to hell." He took a breath. "I love you, Opal Calahan."

"And I think I already showed *you* how I feel. I left my dress rehearsal, because I love you, you big, dumb prospector, letting himself get all arrested..."

A huge, happy laugh escaped him. "Come then, gunslinger girl. Let's catch us a lawman gone bent."

They galloped through the dustbowl-tired grassy

plains around the edge of town to the bridge over the river and Heath's camp. The camp had been trashed: tent ripped, tools everywhere, half his precious mine timbers chopped and smashed.

No sign of the Adder.

He looked over at Opal. A surge of protectiveness smote him. How could he bring her into danger amongst the caves in the mountains?

He opened his mouth, but she read his mind.

"Don't you dare, Heath Rawdon! Don't you go all Australian rugged male on me. You need me. I'm good in a gunfight. Makes my heart beat fast. Makes me feel alive! And if you left me here, I'd just worrit myself into a decline, and then thunder after you anyways, so…"

Laughter bubbled through him. The hell with waiting. Blast finding gold. "Opal, my sweet darling, will you make me the happiest man alive—" He clamped his lips shut.

After.

"Yes, Heath?" So sweet. So seductive. So precious. How could he expose her to certain danger?

Again, she read his thought. She clicked to her horse, leaned forward in the saddle, and started in a fast gallop toward the Medicine Bow Mountain pass.

He hobbled the sheriff's horse, slapped a saddle on Blue, and raced after her.

As he always would.

****

Back in the goldfields, he'd made a couple of Aboriginal mates. More than once, he'd stepped in to even up an unfair fight when gangs of brutal diggers attacked their camp. That didn't endear him to the diggers any, but the Wadawurrung gave him welcome and wattle-seed cakes. His Aboriginal mates warmed him with their sparky humor and intrigued him with their centuries-old bush lore.

They'd taught him some tracking, laughing at his white-fella ignorance. They'd played tricks with marks in soil and bent twigs and grass, until he learned to distinguish faked tracks from genuine.

A pang of homesickness assailed him as he bent to study a boot print in the red soil between stones. Jack and Charlie's wide grins danced in his imagination. Ballarat wasn't all bad. Maybe he'd return one day...

There. A stone shifted from its bed, the fresh exposed soil redder than the surrounding packed, weathered dirt of the trail. Here. The curved rim of a horseshoe imprinted in the shale.

They tracked the bent marshal's trail past Heath's hideout and deeper into the canyon. The pine-scented cliffsides closed in above them. The canyon narrowed into darkness, echoing with eerie silence.

Heath paused, signaling to Opal. "Perfect spot for an ambush." His breath barely tickled the tiny curls at her neck. "Stay behind."

He pulled out his gun and cocked it ready. Held the reins loosely in his left hand. "We don't know far in he is. He's still riding, so we'll stay on our steeds."

Opal nodded. Her holster was strapped over the top of her skirts now, two pistols within quick draw. Heath prayed it wouldn't come to that.

They entered the dark canyon. Heath held up his hand for caution. Sniffed the air. Listened. A dark bird suddenly flew at him from the black depths, cawing loudly. He jerked back with an oath, heart hammering like a mine drill in his chest.

He exhaled fiercely. Sucked in a deep, calming breath. Nudged Blue forward.

They found Adder Jackson's horse tied to a withered tree another mile along the trail. The horse was right down a crease in the trail, down a side slope, under an overhang. If Blue hadn't warned him with a gentle whicker, they would have missed the horse altogether.

They wasted time searching the area for hidden caves. "Let's go on," Heath finally said. "He can't be too far. Stay alert."

"My middle name, cowboy." Opal grinned at him saucily.

His heart melted. So brave. So ebullient. How did a bitter, gloomy individual like him attract such a star maiden?

They tied their horses near Adder's mount, as a tiny trickle of a waterfall gave the horses a drink and sparse grasses would provide tucker until they returned.

Hopefully.

They scrambled up the slope. The canyon tightened here. No room for horses. The path was black and gloomy, filled with strange rustlings. They crept forward, guns out.

"At least," Heath whispered, "you won't shoot me by accident."

Opal's laugh whispered forward. "This is a job for a professional, all right."

A noise just forward. Heath stopped. He sensed Opal right behind him. Quiet and still. Gunslinger mode.

A weak groan emanated from the dark, narrow trail

ahead. *What?*

Some kind of trick maybe. A lure.

"Careful," Heath muttered, and slid forward, every sense pricked and alert, his heart beating a strong, steady beat in his chest and ears.

A flash of light. A soft beam cut the darkness. If the marshal shone a lantern at them, they'd see nothing and he'd see the light reflected from eyes, cheeks and teeth. Heath's form would be outlined within the trail, an easy target. Big enough to block Opal from sight, thankfully.

Heath slunk forward, soft footed, breathing shallowly so the rasp of breath didn't sound in the silence. He flared his nostrils, inhaling cold rock, mountain pine—and the merest hint of leather and sweat.

Another faint groan. Was the Adder injured? Or playing possum?

The weak beam cut the trail again. Coming from a deep side fissure on the right, from the heart of the mountain.

Heath flattened himself against the entrance. He crouched low so he wasn't at eye level and risked a peep around the edge.

The marshal's tall black-clad back was bending over a bundle on the ground. The bundle moved. Groaned.

He had a man in there!

Blood hurtled through Heath's veins. A prick of caution stabbed him, but there was no choice. He motioned Opal to stay put, stepped into the cave, strode forward quickly, trained his gun on the marshal.

Heath flicked a glance to the ragged bundle on the

floor. Flaming hell, the man wore black clothing, black vest, long boots—all he lacked was a silver star. An idea flashed in Heath's brain, but right then, Adder Jackson turned and saw him. Faster than he would have credited, a gun appeared in his hand, jumped, and flashed fire.

Heath slammed behind a long cave pillar as loud echoes rang in the cave and the smell of gunpowder hung heavy.

Another shot. The stalagmite shattered. Heath dropped and rolled. Three quick shots blazed from the cave entrance, and then Opal, blast her proud heart, stepped into the cave.

Heath leaped in front of her as more gunfire split cave stalactites in showers of glowing rainbow shards.

The man on the floor rolled to the rear of the cave. From the depths, he called, voice weak and wavering, but Heath caught every word. "I'm Marshal Adder Jackson. This man is a criminal, wanted across seven counties."

"He lies!" roared the man known to Heath and Opal as Adder. "He's just trying to confuse you. He's the outlaw. I'm bringing him to justice, so get out of my way."

"Call the sheriff," yelled the man on the floor in a strong southern twang. "He'll verify who's the real Adder Jackson, once he asks a few pointy questions."

"Shut up, you," growled the false Adder and pinged off a wild shot to the rear of the cave. Heath heard a soft cry.

He'd heard enough. "Stay hidden, Calahan," he called, hoping the outlaw would think his partner was a man.

Mistake. The false Adder hissed, scorn lashing, "You brought a woman with you, prospector?"

Opal stepped out from a wedge of cave wall and pinged the ground at the marshal's feet.

The gunfight began in earnest. The outlaw sent three shots toward Opal. Pink and orange cave formations exploded in great cracks of sound which echoed through the enclosed space. Masses of shards flew in a colored cloud through the smoke, slicing unprotected skin like tiny knives. The air stank of black powder. Heath snapped shots at the false marshal. "Opal! Get out of here!" he roared.

The outlaw swung at the words, fired. Opal appeared again. Two shots, and the outlaw swore and wrung his right hand as his weapon flew in the air. She took one step forward, stood sideways, ready to peel off another. The outlaw folded over, and then, as if slow motion, rose with another pistol in his left hand. Heath leaped between Opal and the outlaw, she yelled, "No, Heath!" and stepping back into view, fired a slug right into the outlaw's left shoulder.

But the false marshal had got off a shot. Opal teetered sideways and fell flat on the filthy cave floor, littered with sharp flints from the shattered cave formations.

Heath snapped his head back and forth, ran to the outlaw. Kicked the gun from his hand, checked for a pulse. Thready. The outlaw opened his eyes. His mouth twisted in a grin as he stared back at Heath with filmy eyes. "Such is life," he said.

Opal. His heart as splintered as the stalactites, he raced toward her. Pulled her limp form into his arms, rocking and crooning senseless words into her hair.

Then they took shape. "Opal Calahan, I love you, I love you, don't leave me, don't die," he realized he was chanting, over and over.

She opened those crystalline opal eyes and glimmered at him. Her sweet, lovely lips curved in a smile. "I love you too, Heath Rawdon," she said in her delicious voice.

"Don't die, Opal," he begged brokenly. "I love you." The words came in a harsh croak.

She sat up and gave a sunny laugh which ended in a grimace. "It's just my leg, dummy. He shot me in the calf. Couldn't shoot to save himself, that fool."

"Where, where, Opal?" Heath lay her down and hauled up her skirts, running gentle fingers over her bare calves.

"Why, Mr. Rawdon," she said mockingly.

"Don't joke, Opal! Where did he get you?" There! Blood pissing from a nasty wound. He tore a good strip from her frilly petticoat and bound the injury firmly. "That should hold it until I get you back to the doc. I'll take you on my horse."

"I'm fine, Heath," she said, her voice tired and sluggish. Heath regarded her in alarm. How much blood had she lost? "Go and check the real marshal, the real Adder Jackson. See how he is. Crikey, so many things make sense now!"

He found a smile and smoothed her frizzy hair from her heated forehead, beading now with sweat. "Crikey yourself, you gorgeous American gunslinger."

"Go on, Heath. See to the man. Who knows how long the false Adder has kept him here. I'll holler if I'm gonna kick the bucket. But hey, there's plenty sizzle left in me yet, pardner."

Heath cast her a final check over. Nodded.

Walked carefully toward the outlaw. Damn. He should have patted him down, checked for more weapons. He stalked forward. A sudden intent stillness in the false marshal warned him: he ducked and rolled, just as the outlaw stretched his left arm out and snapped off a shot, right where Heath had been standing a mere second ago. Heath's heart nearly exploded through his brain. Red and black ignited in his mind.

He mentally checked himself over. No wound. Shock.

He grabbed a heavy rock and threw it at the outlaw's head. The man grunted. Fired again. Christ, Opal! He could hit her with his wild gunfire. No mercy. He drew his gun. Hesitated. He couldn't shoot a man in cold blood.

He shot the hand holding the gun. The outlaw cursed viciously and released the gun. Pulled his shattered hand against his chest. Heath watched for further movement toward more hidden weapons. Patted the man down. Should have done this earlier.

"Have mercy," the black-eyed outlaw grated. "Shoot me. I can't face justice. Cleaner than a California collar."

Heath hesitated. A strange pang of pity for the outlaw smote him. He could only guess at the circumstances which led to this moment.

"I was a soldier," the man whispered. "War finished, and they turned us out on the world. No work for folk like me. Became a gun for hire." He jerked his head toward Opal. "Saw that chicken when she was a little girl. I shot a man. Working with her famous daddy. Spotted her there, watching in the bushes. Knew she recognized me, but why didn't she say?"

Oh. She'd said Adder Jackson made her stomach shrivel in fear. Something familiar. Well, that mystery was solved.

"Shoot me, one loner, one outsider to another. Finish it."

Compassion stirred hard in Heath. He raised his gun hand.

Chapter Sixteen

The outlaw shut his eyes. Heath slowly pulled back his trigger finger.

Sheriff Branch Wylder's voice echoed in his mind. *"Bring me back a felon under your arm, and you'll get your deputy badge."*

He faced a choice.

A pivotal choice.

His past stretched back. Several futures stretched forward from this moment.

He could choose the old Heath, his old wild life, where men were men and made their own rules. He could shoot this man from a strange kind of kinship of loners.

Or he could choose the law, even though that side had wronged him, had blamed and abandoned him. He could take the outlaw back to the lockup, claim his sheriff's deputy badge. He could support Opal Calahan in her dreams with a regular job. Work his claim before and after work.

Opal. With the greatest luck, Opal Calahan Rawdon.

No choice. It was already made.

He lowered his hand. "I'm sorry, mate. You have crimes to answer for. You can beg the judge at your trial."

A single tear slid from under the outlaw's shut

eyes. "My last bluff. I'm all outta tricks. That's me euchred," he muttered.

The ragged bundle of bones in the rear of the cave twitched as Heath bent over him. "It's over now, Marshal. I'm pleased to meet you. Heath Rawdon, sir."

"I'm mighty pleased to meet you, son. But is that a woman you brought with you?"

"She's a Calahan, sir. The best of them all."

White teeth glimmered. "Untie me, then, and get me out of this thrice-cursed cave."

Heath assisted the marshal to sit. Gave him some water from his flask. "I have to hurry back," Heath told him. "Miss Calahan has a bullet wound in her leg. Can you sit a horse? I can take her with me on my steed if you think you're up to riding."

"Help me stand, son. Let me lean on you outta the cave, and then throw me over the saddle."

Heath carried Opal to the outside of the cave and rested her carefully against the canyon wall, running fingertips under her jaw and holding her wrist to check her elevated pulse. "Will you be all right for a moment, Opal?"

She nodded and gave him a tremulous smile, with the ghost of her usual sauciness dancing in it.

He returned inside for the real Federal Marshal Adder Jackson, who staggered out on unsteady legs, leaning heavily on Heath. He sank down gratefully next to Opal. "Weak as a newborn lamb!" the lawman complained. His eyes glittered. "Fancy that. Me sittin next to a gunslingin' Calahan and never happier in all my born days." They all chuckled, the laughter coming as a rush of welcome relief.

Heath stalked back inside the dark cave, walked to

the rear where a sole lantern still flickered. He stared down at the injured outlaw. "Well, prospector?" the man wheezed, without opening his eyes. "Leave the lantern burn. Don't leave me in the dark, with rats and regrets. Plenty of that where I'm going."

Heath tied the outlaw's legs together securely so he couldn't run, or even crawl, away. Hefted one of the outlaw's guns in his hand, considering.

He placed the pistol on the cave floor near the man's shattered left hand. Growled, "Gun to your left. One bullet in it." He moved it closer with the toe of his boot. "You'd be a determined man to squeeze your broken hand and shoot yourself. One chance. Don't say I've got no mercy in me."

The outlaw's slitted black eyes glittered at him. "More than I woulda done for you, prospector."

Heath inhaled. "I know it, damn you. Here." He leaned down and offered the outlaw a drink from his flask. The man took a few swallows and let the water run down his chin rather than wipe it with either of his broken hands.

Heath rasped, "I'll be back with the Wylder sheriff soon. An hour, maybe. You'll be arrested and dragged back in chains to face trial for your crimes."

The outlaw's lips twisted. He grunted, "Don't hurry back." He opened his eyes and stared back up at Heath all snap gone. Defeated. "I'll see you in hell."

Heath rose, took a step.

"Prospector."

He turned back. Let the dying man hurl curses at him one final time.

"An old miner told me you got...gemstones..."

Heath snapped to attention. Bent and gave the man

more water. "Marshal?" Hard to call him anything else.

"Next the riverbank…near the old tree. He couldn't make it back to dig…"

The outlaw lapsed into unconsciousness.

Heath covered him in one of the blankets the real marshal had been wrapped in. Poetic justice, he supposed. He grabbed rope coiled in an alcove and another blanket to roll under Opal's injured leg.

Now, he had to get her and the genuine marshal to a doctor, and fast.

Outside, he checked their vital signs once again, saw Opal was bleeding through her bandage. He ran down the canyon path, slipping and sliding on the loose rubble, stones pinging down the steep canyon side. Panic shouted in his frantic brain. He grabbed the horses, Blue and the sheriff's beast, coaxed, pulled, and persuaded them into the narrow, dark canyon path.

The lawman was too frail and sick from long imprisonment to sit a horse properly, so Heath tied him to the saddle, looping Marshal Jackson's hands into the reins. He lifted Opal up onto Blue, careful not to bang her injured leg, although she stifled a sharp cry twice. He tied the marshal's horse behind Blue.

Sweating with urgency, he mounted smoothly behind his gunslinger and headed back to Wylder.

****

Heath pushed out his chest, a world of strange emotions grabbing him by the throat and choking him. Opal clapped her hands prettily, crutches propped next to her seat.

Sheriff Branch Wylder made a short, formal speech. "Welcome to the law-keeping force of Wylder, Heath Rawdon. Glad you've come over to the side of

217

right and justice. You've proved your mettle by seizing a notorious outlaw, and the folk of seven counties will be singing your name for years to come." He held up a badge theatrically. Pinned the silver deputy's star to Heath's vest.

The small audience squeezed into the sheriff's tiny office applauded loudly and cheered. Miss Delphina Mathilde Treadway stamped her cane and called, "Bravo!" Molly Maguire and Parkinson had bustled over from the Vincent. Bluebell jumped up and shouted in excitement. Even Cissy and Buck Standish had come to pay their respects. Buck stepped forward and slapped Heath's shoulders in a gesture of solidarity—two men choosing the right path so they could make a life with their astonishing women. The Wylder newspaper man scribbled notes and then bustled out to write his story. The crowd filed out.

"And now, children," Sheriff Wylder drawled, a huge grin stretching his mouth, "I got a surprise." He nodded at Opal. "This might come in handy, Miss Calahan. There's a reward in five counties for the capture of Wild Sam the Smasher. Five thousand dollars."

What? A fantastic, life-changing sum. Opal's luscious mouth dropped open.

"He was dead when we all got back there, Sheriff. Sir." Heath attempted his new respectful tone.

The sheriff shut one eye and peered at him. "Something wrong with your digestion, Deputy?"

"Trying on the respect, sir. Need practice."

The sheriff laughed. "That reward is for *dead or alive*, Deputy."

Heath met Opal's glowing gaze.

218

In a way, Heath wished he'd known the outlaw before he got too violent and wild, killing men and kidnapping a marshal so he could assume his identity.

Somehow, that man had found the balls to grab the gun in his shattered hand and shoot himself right between the eyebrows. A last act of desperate courage.

Heath wasn't sorry. "I'll wear my new badge to Opal's play tonight."

"You certainly will, Deputy. You are on duty. Your first assignment."

Heath shook the sheriff's hand.

Chapter Seventeen

The play was planned, prepared, and ready. Excitement hurtled so fast and fizzing under Opal's skin, she felt like a ripe fruit, full of juice and ready to burst.

There was a time to be hasty—like breaking the man you love out of wrongful arrest in the lockup—and a time to be steady and cautious.

Like designing and delivering your second play.

Everything depended on tonight.

Opal stood, supporting the shaking arm of Miss Delphina Mathilde, staring at the theater. "Glorious!" the old lady whispered, awed.

The old music hall lived once more, transformed into the magnificent, glittering Wylder Playhouse. Heath and his new cowboy deputy friends had worked night and day to get the theater glowing and gorgeous, although Heath did slink off to his claim every now and again, a preoccupied expression on his face.

The playhouse's front glistened with new paint. Great wide white steps, clean and gleaming, reflected golden light streaming from its many windows, promising magic. Music floated on the air and curled down the street, calling the folk of Wylder to come and be entertained.

A huge laughing, jostling queue of western folk in their very finest gear waited to be admitted. Jewels glittered; moustaches gleamed in waxed glory; high curled hairstyles and low necklines mocked gravity; laughter bubbled like champagne.

Opal and Miss Treadway entered via a side door, then stationed themselves inside the entrance to the theater, sparkling with light. Around the walls, within the heavy gilded frames of the restored pictures, a young, glamorous Delphina Mathilde Treadway smiled seductively.

The great doors were thrown open. The crowd surged forward.

Opal Calahan and Miss Delphina Mathilde greeted each person as they showed their ticket, welcoming them to the new Wylder Playhouse.

Her heart felt so full she thought she might cry. Or laugh. Instead, she smiled her hugest grin, clasping hands, bestowing air kisses, shooting delighted smiles at her patron between greeting each guest.

So many people she loved were in the audience. Her youngest brother Neddy had finally arrived in Wylder, miraculously still intact, not injured, maimed, nor killed. He'd kissed Opal, whispered, "Hey, sis. I wouldn't miss your triumph for the world." Cissy Standish, heavily pregnant, had carefully lowered herself into a front row seat next to Neddy, Buck hovering anxiously. Many of the Vincent staff had been given the time off, provided they rushed back to cater for the thirsty theater crowd immediately after. Even the giggling women from the Wylder County Social Club had arrived, adding an exotic, perfumed glamor to the playhouse audience. Cowboys packed in as tight as their pistols.

The music increased into a crescendo, trumpets

soaring and drums crashing. Lights dimmed. Whispers and laughter rose and settled into silence. The great doors closed.

Let the play begin.

It all started so well. Miss Delphina Mathilde commanded the stage from the instant she stepped into the spotlight. Gone was the shaking old lady, and instead a dignified grande dame first grabbed the audience's attention, then charmed and bespelled them as she sang and performed a wobbling dance.

Bluebell swallowed her nerves and recited her lines perfectly. Leading man Buck Standish was a fine, heroic figure. Opal could hear half the ladies in the audience sighing amorously. Even the Sagebrush triplets performed magnificently, charming sudden applause from the audience with their cute antics. The heavy red stage curtains opened and closed and opened again on cue.

Opal crossed nervous fingers behind her back.

Dared she hope…?

Too soon. Bluebell staggered. Screamed. Fell to the floor. Buck stood frozen for a moment, then rose magnificently to the occasion, scooping Bluebell in his arms and carrying her off the stage to resounding applause. Opal signaled wildly.

The young cowboys acting as stagehands at last got the message. The stage curtains shut to thunderous applause.

Opal hobbled to the actors' room to find Miss Treadway fanning herself in a chair. Bluebell sat nearby, foot elevated on a stool, thin face streaked with tears. Neddy was carefully strapping her ankle.

When she saw Opal, she tried to jump up, but

Neddy held her firm. "None of that now, Miss Bluebell. You done sprained that ankle. That's the end of your actin' tonight."

Opal's heart absolutely sank in her chest. "No!" she cried, then immediately felt terrible as fresh tears sprouted from her assistant's white, stricken face. "Bluebell, please don't worry."

"The play must go on." She cast her gaze around. "Where's our understudy? The Vincent Hotel maid, Sally Eccleston?"

"Not well, Miss Opal," Bluebell whispered. "Nauseous with nerves. I didn't want to worry you. I told her to head off home."

Good grief, who could she summon at a moment's notice? "Blast! Why didn't I organize a second understudy? Opal, you *fool*."

"You do it, Miss Opal."

"What? No. I'm the director. Plus I'm leaning on a walking stick."

"You know all the lines word perfect. You, with your pretty face and elegant form. *You can do it*."

Opal stared at her.

Her assistant nodded. "There's all kinds of bravery, Miss Opal. I reckon you're blessed with nearly all of 'em."

She squared her shoulders. Nodded. Inhaled. "I'll be leading lady. Bluebell, ask my obliging and very clever brother to shift you a chair to the wings where you can see the action." She smoothed her young assistant's hair. "You can whisper the lines if I forget."

Bluebell brightened. Opal knew all the lines word perfect, of course, but now Bluebell would feel she still had a vital role and would stop dwelling on her mishap.

Forget to blame herself.

Opal flittered around and informed all the actors. Everyone was ready.

She sent the sheriff to the stage to announce a change in personnel due to a slight accident. "Not to worry," he said to the house in his easy manner. "Madam Playwright herself will be leading lady."

The playhouse echoed with excited applause. "See?" Bluebell hissed. "They love you already."

The second act proceeded apace. Opal and Buck were just about to enact a passionate scene, when a scream shattered the theater's entranced silence.

Oh no. What disaster threatened now?

Cissy Standish half rose from her seat. "Buck," she called softly. "Buck!" She yelped. "Arrrgh! Buck, I believe the baby is coming."

Her leading man vaulted from the stage and landed before the front row seats. He wrapped Cissy in his arms. People stood up, craning their necks to see. Some folk stood on their seats, the better to see the next drama being played out in the audience seats. The noise rose as the patrons asked each other in loud voices what had happened. Opal's brother and two sheriff's deputies cleared a path for the couple, Buck half carrying Cissy, until they could exit the playhouse.

"Go call them a carriage," Opal whispered to one of her stagehands. The lad vanished.

She'd never thought Buck could let her down. No understudy. She'd never planned on the baby coming.

Opal stood irresolute on the stage, her playwright dreams fragmenting in tatters and shards all around her feet. A second drama disaster? Folk would never pay to see her plays again. She'd be mocked, derided, and run out of town.

She and Neddy would have to become gunslingers for hire.

A few speeches. Another couple of songs. That's all she could give the hungry audience now. She knew after last time what crowds were like. One moment in the palm of your hand, and the next an angry, heaving mob, screaming abuse and baying for blood.

She girded herself to make the call.

And then…

Heath Rawdon, the man who hated and feared playhouses, who got dire flashbacks from the night his mate went missing two years ago in Ballarat, walked strong and tall through the milling, restive crowd.

She watched him, holding her breath.

Heath stepped long-legged right up onto the stage, out from the darkness and into the spotlight. He took Opal's free hand in his own calloused fingers. Waited until the grumbling, heaving mob settled and became an audience once more.

And he took right over from where Buck left off.

Word perfect.

He knew every phrase. Every scene. Every stage direction.

The dramatic second act drew to a close. Without a single hitch. Followed by the third act. Smooth and wonderful. Exactly how she'd imagined.

The audience gave them a standing ovation at the finale, clapping and cheering, hollering praise and jokes, demanding encores and bows. Near the front, even helmet woman's eyes shone with tears as she applauded. Perhaps she had a mote in there.

At the third bow, Heath drew Opal to the front of

the stage.

"Heath," she whispered. She dropped her stick, gripped both his hands, and glowed at him with everything she had. "You saved me. You gave me back my dream. I don't know what it cost you." Tears sprang in her eyes. "Thank you."

Heath kept hold of her right hand and turned to the audience. "Good folk of Wylder. I'm Heath Rawdon. Goldfields scum. Restless, abandoned, unloved." He paused. The audience held its collective breath.

"And then I met a unique, brave, extraordinary, gunslinging woman who had a marvelous dream. You've just seen this dream come alive." Scattered claps. Heath held up a commanding hand. "In a moment," he growled. "First, I want to say this.

"Miss Opal Calahan does not let anyone define who she is. She makes her own choices, allows her heart and quick brain to guide her true. She chooses to love me. Me, Heath Rawdon, for reasons which I will never understand." Laughter. Hoots and catcalls.

"Because of her love, I'm a changed man. I'm now a proud sheriff's deputy. On the right side of the law."

Loud applause. "Right now, I need an answer to a question. I'm hoping the answer will make me the happiest man alive."

He turned to Opal. What she saw there, burning in his haunted dark eyes, filled her heart to overflowing.

"Miss Opal Calahan, I love you with every fiber of my being. I love your opal eyes, your frizzy, mad hair. I love your slender, strong body. I love your true, courageous heart and mercurial, smart brain. Could you love me? Opal, will you marry me? Let me adore you and cherish you as long as we both shall live."

Huge noise. Tins rattling, cheering, suggested answers ripe with innuendo hollered. People stood in their chairs and threw flowers at the couple, glowing in a full spotlight now, aimed at them by the mischievous stagehands.

Heath waited. The great hall fell silent.

"I got flaws, Heath. I'm hasty. I'm a gunslinger. But maybe those parts of me are who I am. I'll try not to be too madcap. I'll try not to shoot anybody—unless they threaten someone I love. Sure you want me, Heath Rawdon?"

"What a time to show caution! I'm dreaming of a little *hastiness* right now, Opal."

The whole hall shook with laughter, then fell silent in held-breath anticipation.

She stuttered a laugh; her heart felt full to overflowing and about to blow apart all at once.

Heath said, "My Opal. My precious, lovely, adored Miss Opal Calahan." He squeezed her shoulders with his warm, steady palms. Gently rubbed her upper arms.

His deep voice anchored her. "Be proud, Opal. You are unique. Passionate. With handy skills in a crisis! Courageous and creative. I love *all* of who you are."

"Yes," said hasty, happy Opal Calahan. "I love you with every fiber of my being, Heath Rawdon. I want nothing more than to become your wife. I hope to bear our little goldmining, gunslinging babies. Yes. Oh, yes."

The hall erupted as they kissed. The folk of Wylder surged onto the stage and picked up Heath and Opal, lifted them aloft, and carried them triumphantly out into Wylder Street.

Held high in the air by many arms, Heath and Opal

linked hands and gazed into each other's beloved faces, laughing.

****

Much later, Heath took Opal back to his camp.

There in the desert, they danced together under the moonlight, serenaded by owls and night herons.

"I've something to show you," Heath said, his deep voice sending delighted shivers tickling under her skin.

"That sounds promising." She used her best breathy whisper and watched his eyes darken.

"Come." He led her to the riverbank and helped her to clamber down a new, shallow mine shaft leading from the bank.

He turned the lantern to a thin beam.

Something glittered blue, green, and turquoise in the rock. "Opal," he growled. "We've found opal. That false marshal told me about it. After I left him the gun. So he could end it fast."

She traced slow fingertips over the glowing gems. "Oh, its magical. Bewitching," she breathed. "What exquisite colors."

"Not as beautiful as my Opal."

His lips met hers. They kissed, there in the damp and dirt, Heath backing her against the wall, pulling her to his body. "Turned out opal is lucky for me after all."

The sound of approaching hoofbeats floated on the evening air. They both froze.

"The false marshal is dead and gone," Opal said.

They climbed from the mine to see the shadowy figure of a tall man astride a horse loom into view. Heath pulled Opal behind him.

"Deputy."

Heath relaxed. Sheriff Branch Wylder. The

lawman said, "News from Ballarat just in."

Ballarat! Every muscle in Heath wound tight. An invisible hand gripped his throat. Black roaring screamed in his ears—then softened into silence. He was no longer that man.

The document in the sheriff's hand shone pale in the evening gloaming.

Heath waited a beat. Took the paper. His whole future…

He cleared his throat and read it aloud, hearing his own voice shake. "We can confirm that the Morning Star claim, Ballarat, was on the night of 26 May 1877, taken by bushrangers, gold stolen, and the man guarding the claim, one Daniel Lonigan, also kidnapped by same bushrangers. Dan Lonigan was held with the outlaws for some time, until he effected an escape. Lonigan is hale and well and living in Castlemaine. All theft, murder, and larceny charges against Heath Rawdon are formally dropped throughout Ballarat and western Victoria."

His gaze shot to the sheriff, who scratched his head and grinned from ear to ear. "You're a free man, Deputy Rawdon."

Heath gazed at Opal, his heart overflowing. She ran to him and gripped his hands tight.

He rasped, "Not any more I'm not, Sheriff." Her smile dazzled. "I will have a gorgeous wife—" His voice cracked. "—and *children* to support."

Right there in front of the beaming sheriff, Heath caught Opal in his arms, swung her around, and kissed her soundly.

A word about the author...

Maryanne Ross writes historical romance with sparkle and steam, lively heroines and rugged heroes.

Victorians Unlaced series:
Crushing the Corset—A young female hotelier fights for her inheritance against her wicked uncle, with only a mysterious highwayman to aid her, on the North York Moors, UK.
Bouncing the Bustle—A female plant collector in the Tasmanian wilderness sparks up against a rugged wildlife rescuer.
Coming soon: *Pitching the Petticoat*—A Scottish bluestocking meets a sword-fighting hero with secrets.

Wylder West series: *Wylder Opal*—an action-and romance-packed western with a gunslinger heroine.

Maryanne also writes contemporary romance and award-winning short crime fiction. In *How (Not) to Make a Grandchild*, a female landscape gardener falls for a construction boss.
Maryanne loves bushwalking and traveling with her own romantic hero. She works as a PR and development consultant for an Aboriginal organization.

Check out her books and connect with Maryanne at
https://www.maryanneross.com/
https://www.facebook.com/MaryanneRossAuthor

Thank you for purchasing
this publication of The Wild Rose Press, Inc.

For questions or more information
contact us at
info@thewildrosepress.com.

The Wild Rose Press, Inc.
www.thewildrosepress.com